Finding Faith

By Reana Malori

Editor: April Allen

Summary

Cooper Branson wasn't ready to move on. His life was just fine the way it was and no one could make him change. At least, not willingly. He wore his Widower badge with honor and forced himself to live his life only for his daughter, Madison. Falling for his attractive neighbor was not in the cards for him. It didn't matter that she was the first person he thought of in the morning, or the last voice he needed to hear before falling asleep at night. Loving someone and running the risk of losing them again was not a risk he was willing to take.

Faith Douglas was ready to reinvent herself. After a hurtful betrayal by her closest friend, Faith was determined to live life for herself. The first step to her new outlook on life was doing something she would have never done before. Walking across the lawn and saying hello to her new, hunky neighbor was the bravest thing she had done in a long time. How was she to know that the man would become her world and his daughter would steal her heart? What she never expected was to stand in the shadow of another woman while the man she loved looked right through her.

Finding out who you are, while ignoring the expectations of others, is the toughest path anyone can take. Cooper and Faith have to decide if they're able to move on from the hurt of the past to find their future.

Finding Faith
Table of Contents

Chapter One

"I don't know why you thought that man ever wanted you in the first place. I'm more his type anyway. I think he just took pity on you until he could get to me," the hurtful words spewed from the mouth of the woman sitting across from her.

"Excuse me? What did you just say?" Faith Douglas almost choked on her ice tea. The words stunned her and she was almost certain that she must have heard incorrectly. Almost.

Her jaw had gone slack at how the conversation had turned so negative, so quickly. Her mind had become numb with shock as she tried to process what had just happened. She felt unable to move or respond, as if anchored in place and chained down to her chair. This unexpected nastiness coming at her from the woman sitting across the table felt like it had to be a bad joke.

"Well, I'm just saying." Denise turned her head and watched the two handsome, well-dressed men walk out of the restaurant. "I'm sure I'll be hearing from them both later today. The one with the goatee couldn't keep his eyes off of me," she said with a smirk.

"Okay, not sure what the hell that's all about, but you can have them both. I had no interest in either of them," Faith responded before taking a sip of her drink and giving herself a moment to take a breath. "This was supposed to be a casual lunch anyway. Why did you invite them to sit down?" Faith's voice held a distinct chill. If Denise had been listening close enough, she would have heard this.

It almost felt as if she was having an out of body experience. Today was supposed to be about two old friends reconnecting and getting together for lunch, but it had turned into something she never would have expected. For the past six months, work had become even busier and she had fallen into an endless loop of wake-up, go to work, drive home, eat dinner, work some more, and go to sleep, so this has seemed like a good idea.

"You know, Faith, if you would only lose some weight, men might want you more." Her gaze traveled up and down Faith's form as she tilted her head in a look that could only be interpreted as pity. "I mean, damn, girl, look at you. Your face is pretty enough, but you have too much ass and thighs for a man to really want to do anything with you. Your stomach pooches and I can see a second chin starting to form." A look of feigned sadness crossed her features, "I mean, you should really take better care of yourself. Hell, you probably have cobwebs down there." Laughing at her own mean and callous joke at her friend's expense, Denise seemed oblivious to the pain and hurt that resulted from her words.

Taking a few deep breaths, Faith tried to calm herself before she said something that couldn't be taken back. After a few seconds, she gave up the fight. There was no way in hell this was happening. Not today. To anyone looking at her, they would have seen eyes half-closed in anger, her cheeks a dark burgundy as she tried to quell her embarrassment, and body language that communicated pure outrage.

“Are you done insulting me?” The questioning look on Denise’s face almost took Faith over the edge. “How dare you assume that I would want any advice from you? Whatsoever. Regarding anything. Let alone, my weight?” Her face must have betrayed her complete shock and outrage. Hell, she was just downright pissed.

“Well, I’m just saying.” Flipping her feathered and curled hair over her shoulders and briefly looking at her perfectly manicured nails, the two-faced woman must have had a lack of oxygen to the brain, because she clearly didn't know when to shut her mouth. “Maybe if you worked out a little more or at least dressed like you wanted a man, you might actually get one.”

Faith’s response was swift and left no room for interpretation. “Have you lost your damn mind? Where is this coming from, Denise? I’m not even sure why you would fix your mouth to say this to me.” Reaching over to grab her purse, she began to gather her things. If she did not leave soon, she could not be held accountable for what happened next.

Stopping to look at Faith as if she were imparting some great wisdom, the haughty look on her face was almost funny, if the situation wasn't so damn sad. “Trust me, honey, no man wants to wrap his arms around a woman that's bigger than him. Plus, do you really think real men enjoy being with a woman that everyone thinks of as a Big…Beautiful...Woman?” She said the words slowly, almost as if it were distasteful. That just pissed Faith off even more.

The anger simmering just under the surface was about to cause Faith to go back to her roots on this chick, and quickly. Normally, she was a quiet woman who allowed most things to roll off of her back. “Like a duck” was one of her favorite sayings and that's what she had become known for. Unfortunately, some people took her kindness for weakness and most times, that was okay.

Over the years, she had used that assumption to reel them in and once they were in a state of relaxation, believing they had won, she unleashed her full fury on them. Not many things took her to that point and keeping her cool had become almost an art. But this was simply too much and her cup had runneth over with the bullshit coming out of this woman's mouth. Faith was done.

While she would never claim to be model thin or even skinny, being a size fourteen—sixteen on an off day—was not necessarily considered a big beautiful woman, or BBW. Not that there was anything wrong with it, but why would she simply put up with someone placing a label on who she was? Never one to be put in a box built by someone else, she had never responded well to other people telling her what she should think, or how she should feel.

Maybe some people would call her fat or overweight, or whatever the hell they wanted to say about her pants size, but that had never factored into how she felt about herself. Working out regularly was a part of her normal weekly routine. She visited the gym at her office at least three times a week, walking or jogging on the treadmill, or gliding on the elliptical machine for at least forty-five minutes every visit.

Yes, she was pleasantly plump, but what the hell did that have to do with anything? Did that give another person the right to say anything to her and belittle her without provocation? Standing at five feet nine inches, with golden brown skin and luscious curves, she was more than enough woman for the right man. There were plenty of men who looked at her with lust and desire in their eyes. Every single damn day. And, yes, she ate it up every time. No, a lack of self-esteem or body issues would never have entered the conversation if it were up to her. Clearly, Denise was the one with the issue, not Faith.

Deciding that now was the right time to end this conversation, she addressed the woman sitting across from her, "Denise, let me stop you right there." Teeth clenched tight, her voice was strained as she tried to control herself and not make a scene in a public place. Heat radiated from her body and she knew her eyes must be shooting fire right now.

"I'm not sure what made you think that today was the time and place for you to lecture me on how I look or the shape of my body. How I look is none of your damn business." She could feel her hands beginning to shake as she barely controlled the urge to smack the smug look off her former friend's face.

A fabricated look of shock and surprise came over the other woman's face as Faith laid into her. The entire facade was completely lost on Faith and it was really quite pathetic. At one time, Faith would have wanted nothing more than to look more like the woman sitting across from her. The long wavy hair, the thin, but shapely body, and the upturned hazel eyes. There was no shame in stating that Denise was a very beautiful woman. But today, she had become someone very ugly on inside. Her once beautiful face had transformed into something quite hideous.

She and Denise had known one another since their college years, when they were both two young freshman trying to find their way in this big, bad world. Supporting each other through successes, failures, relationships, and long days when only a pint of ice cream would make it better, had become the norm. That was simply what they did for each other. That relationship had meant so much to her as the years had passed, and now, in one afternoon, it had been burned to the ground.

"Faith, girl, what are you talking about? I'm just trying to keep it real. You know how we do." If she could truly believe her friend's intentions were real and true, then Faith would have backed off in a heartbeat. But something about the words were hurtful and tinged with a whole lot of cruelty. No, this had definitely been intentional.

"No, Denise. You're not keeping it real. Why you choose today to tell me how you really feel about me, I'll never know. But now that I see the real you, all I can say is thank you." Shaking her head at the feeling of betrayal coursing through her veins, Faith continued, "Thank you for showing me that you had been faking all these years. Thank you for freeing me from a friendship that was as fake as those damn nails on your fingers."

Denise seemed to finally sense that she had gone too far, "Faith, you're being entirely too sensitive. You know I've always told you that you were kind of big and needed to lose some weight." Glancing away from Faith for a second, Denise smiled at a handsome man standing across the room at the hostess stand, but his gaze never captured hers.

Faith watched the interaction and noticed that the man seemed to look everywhere but at Denise. There was no interest whatsoever. And then it hit her. Yes, this was about her and the way she looked, but not the way she had initially thought. Understanding hit her like a brick.

Voice raised, she confronted Denise with her new found knowledge, "Is this because of that bullshit party we went to a few weeks ago?" At the sudden turning of her head to look at Faith, the truth of her words were confirmed.

Faith continued, unable to hold the words back, "Are you fucking kidding me right now? You're coming at me with claws bared because of a man? A man whom you hardly knew. A man that I had absolutely no interest in."

Denise's face suddenly turned ugly with rage and hate as she snarled her next words, "What the fuck ever, Faith! You knew that I was going after him, but you just had to swing your big, fat ass in his direction. I don't even know why I brought you to that party anyway. You weren't even invited."

"What is that supposed to mean," she questioned. Had she ever really known this person at all?

"It means I only brought you with me out of pity. Did you not see the people in the room?" Snidely, she looked at Faith with a look akin to disgust, "You were clearly out of your league. I have no idea why a man would be interested enough in you to spend two hours talking to you at a party full of beautiful women. You would never fit into his world and men like that only want women like you for a booty call. An experience. Nothing more."

Damn, this was some cold shit. "I never knew you at all, did I? All these years, you thought you were doing me a favor by being my friend? Did you really think I needed you to help my self-image?" Pausing for a second to get her bearings, Faith started to laugh. She laughed at all the time she had wasted on trying to be a good friend. She laughed about the utter gall of the woman sitting in front of her.

She was jealous. The vitriol coming out of her mouth could only be explained by that one undeniable fact. Laughing harshly at the utter stupidity of her former friend, she noticed the looks and glances from the other patrons of the restaurant. Sitting across from her with crossed arms, Denise's body was tense and stiff. She seemed baffled by what was going on, and Faith almost felt pity for her.

Her laughing slowly came to a halt and she wiped her eyes. Steeling her voice, she spoke to Denise as her friend for the last time, "How about this, from this point forward, you focus on you and I will focus on me." Gathering her purse that had fallen to the side during their argument, she prepared to leave the restaurant and return to the office. This lunch had turned out to be a very bad idea. "You have let your jealousy ruin a friendship that lasted for more than fifteen years. What you did today was petty and spiteful and I will never forget what you said to me. If you see me on the street, keep on walking. From this point forward, we are strangers. Keep your distance."

Standing up from the table, she dug into her purse, pulled out some bills from her wallet, and threw them onto the table. "I may have a few extra pounds on me, but I know who and what I am. I will never allow envy or jealousy to turn me into an ugly person. Too bad you never learned that lesson."

Walking away with her head held high, Faith exited the restaurant and breathed in the crisp air of the nation's capital. She loved living in Washington,

DC. There was no other place like it and she loved the feel and pace of the city. The diversity of the people walking around her was welcomed. Various shades of skin color, some in suits, others in jeans, tall, short, skinny and not-so-skinny, and people from every walk of life.

Thinking back on the scene in the restaurant, she shook her head in frustration. More times than not, it had always been Denise who had thrown Faith a nugget of "reality" when a good looking man had been interested in her. Or when she wanted to buy a more risqué outfit to wear out for a night of fun, Denise usually said just the right words to make her place the item back on the store rack.

Her pitying looks and statements of, "I don't know if he's serious about you. I didn't want to say anything, but I saw him looking at other women while standing right next to you," all came flooding back. Damn, she had been so stupid. Everyone hears about the backstabbing friends who make every effort to undermine you, but she never thought Denise would be one of them.

Raising her arm in the air in the universal signal to hail a cab, Faith was determined to put the hateful things Denise had said behind her. She didn't need friends like that anyway. She had her books and her work and she was happy. Well, as happy as one could be without close friends, a boyfriend, children and an entire life that seemed to revolve around work.

Chapter Two

Three days later, Faith was sitting on her chaise in the living room, watching a marathon of her favorite crime show featuring a diverse group of FBI agents. It was easy to get lost in this show and all the craziness of the bad people they hunted in a one-hour episode. Looking over at her cell phone, she sighed loudly. It had been difficult to stop herself from calling Denise after work yesterday. Although they hadn't seen each other much over the past months, they always managed to speak on the phone for a few minutes after a long week of work. It had felt natural to pick up her phone and begin to dial her number. That was, until she remembered the hurtful words that had come out of her mouth just a few days ago.

Just this morning after having her first cup of coffee, Faith had committed to finding herself, to understanding who she was. Not who she was based on her degrees, title, or the company she worked for. Not even who or what her family and friends expected her to be—and God knows—they all had an opinion. No, it was time for her to build her own path. Find her own way. And she was focused on doing it on her own terms.

Watching the credits from the third show in a day-long marathon scroll across the screen, she realized it was good to just do her own thing and not worry about what was going on with anyone else. As Faith was about to get up and refill her glass of lemonade, she heard the unmistakable noise of a moving truck pulling into the driveway of the house next door. Her new neighbors were finally moving in.

Having visited the house next door a few times, she always felt that it was a beautiful home. Larger than most homes in the cul-de-sac, it had the feel of a family home. One that had been made for children to grow up in and thrive. Just two months ago, the former owners had put the house up for sale when the wife was offered a promotion. It came with a move to another state and a huge salary increase. Luckily for them, the husband was able to get a job transfer to the same location, so they packed up their kids and belongings and headed out west.

They had been a friendly couple, but because she was single without a boyfriend or significant other, they didn't get together all that often. Just for general group gatherings or when the wife tried to set Faith up with one of her husband's friends. Her heart had always been in the right place and some of them had been the perfect catch, for anyone but her.

Opening her curtains a bit more, she glanced out of the window and noticed a tall, blond man with an athletic build exiting a new model black SUV. "Now that is a one fine ass man! His wife is one lucky woman."

Craning her neck to get a better look, she guessed he had to be at least six feet two inches tall, and with a physique like that, his workout regimen had to be brutal. Even from this distance and seeing him in casual clothing, she doubted there was an ounce of fat on his body. It was Saturday, he was moving into a new home, and his clothing reflected a man ready for some hard work. He was outfitted in well-worn jeans that fit him like a second skin, with a black t-shirt emblazoned with the U.S. Army logo across the front.

Taking her time to look him over, especially since he hadn't yet seen her, she also noticed that he was very confident in both his actions and demeanor. The movers weren't polished men, but he looked comfortable speaking with them. Not everyone could do that, but given his choice of clothing, maybe he was current or former military. Having never served in the military, she knew people from all walks of life joined and she heard that you gained the ability to be comfortable in any environment. It was like they were trained to act like a chameleon, changing their personality, tone, and behaviors to fit their surroundings.

As he stood unmoving for a few moments next to his truck, a few more cars pulled up to the house. Maybe she would catch a glimpse of the wife. Rising to her toes, she balanced one hand on the wall next to her, just next to the window. So maybe she was a little nosey. Oh, well. It was important to know who was living next to you. After a few moments, she could see an older couple exit one car, while another older woman exited a second car alone. They greeted each other like old friends. "Must be the parents," she commented to herself.

The third car held another couple, who stepped out of their car and smiled up at her new neighbor. It was a younger couple. A tall white man, a short, thin, but curvy black woman, and a little girl with light skin and curly, light brown hair. Her new neighbor lifted his arm, waving to them just as something in his vehicle caught his eye. Smiling, he yelled out something to the younger couple and made his way to the back of the truck, opening the back door. Watching him lean in, she stood rooted to the spot as she saw a little girl, no more than four or five years old, run across the yard and over to the other little girl, giving her a big hug as they began to chat away. "Hmmm, where's the wife?"

Getting a little too nosey, she pulled the curtain back a little too much and the motion must have been noticed before she was able to steady herself. Her new neighbor and the younger couple all turned their heads toward her house, watching the window for a sign of any other movement. While the couple looked in her direction for a few more seconds, they quickly turned back to watching the two little girls. Her sexy neighbor on the other hand continued to watch the window for a few moments longer. Although her rational mind knew he couldn't see her, she couldn't prevent the thought that he could see inside and was aware that she had been staring at him.

"Smooth move, Faith. Staring at a man moving into the house next door, and one who is clearly taken. Yup, you've lost it." Even this was said in a whisper. Yup, she was definitely watching too much of this marathon. Maybe it was time to put on a comedy. What must he think of his new neighborhood now that she had behaved like a typical nosey busybody?

One of the older ladies came over to him and touched his arm, saying something to him and the other people milling around. Turning his gaze away from the front of her house to respond, he then motioned for everyone to move toward the house. Taking one more glance in her direction, he turned and started walking toward his new home. Faith quickly moved back from the window. Hoping that she hadn't been caught again, she knew her luck had already run out. As she thought about what had just occurred, her lips started quivering and she burst out in laughter.

"Well, damn. Now I have to go introduce myself. Make a peace offering and all that jazz." Slowly turning away from the window, she went into her kitchen and pulled out the makings for a simple pasta casserole.

"I just hope he doesn't tell his wife that they have a weirdo next door neighbor who doubles as a peeping Tom." Never good at meeting new people, she was nervous about making the first move. But if she didn't do it soon, she would lose her nerve and she would find herself too embarrassed to cross that bridge at a later date.

No, she had to do this. After all, she had made a promise to herself to do more things that were completely out of character. It was time for Faith to find herself.

∞ ∞ ∞ ∞ ∞

"Okay, baby, stay here for just a few minutes while daddy gets this taken care of." Cooper Branson turned toward the backseat as he spoke to his four-year old daughter.

"Okay, daddy. But, is Bree coming over to see my new house today?" Looking in the backseat at his little girl, he knew this had been the right thing for them. This move was going to be a good thing. It was time for a fresh start.

"Yes, baby, her parents are bringing her right now" he responded lovingly. "They were right behind your grandma. She'll be here in just a few minutes and then I'll take you out of your seat. Okay?"

"Okay," his daughter responded. Within seconds she was playing with her pink and purple polka-dot notebook and drawing squiggly lines that only she knew the meaning of.

Stepping out of his SUV, Cooper ran a hand down his face. Damn, he was exhausted. Looking at the house in front of him and the surrounding neighborhood, he knew that this is where they needed to be. Inside, he knew that at this moment, he belonged here.

Without warning, a tingling feeling in his stomach started to make itself known. He stilled for a few seconds as awareness of what that meant sank in. There was no reason why he should be getting a feeling that something momentous was about to occur. Unless it was just the change in environment and the general move. It was a new home for him and his daughter, so that could explain it.

Plus, he hadn't felt something this strong in his gut since the day his wife had died. Quickly looking over at the car where his daughter sat, he forced himself to calm his racing heart. "She's fine, Cooper," he whispered under his breath.

Inhaling deeply, he pointedly ignored the feeling. He had to remember that he was not overseas fighting with insurgents, nor could he live his life constantly expecting the other shoe to drop.

Excitement and sadness warred within him as he tried to get his mind prepared for the task in front of him. Today was going to be a good day. Hell, every day he had in front of him would be better than the one before it. Nothing, and no one, could tell him that this wasn't the right choice. It had been almost four years since his wife had died and it had simply been time for change.

More than anyone, he knew that living in their old home had kept him trapped in a never-ending loop of reliving every memory they had made together. Sleeping in their bedroom had become torture. Her smell lingered. Her voice whispered to him from every corner of the room. Memories of every moment they had lived together within those four walls had almost strangled him. Eventually, just so that he could get a good night's sleep, he had moved to the vacant guest room.

Every morning as he took a shower, images of their lovemaking would roll through his mind like a movie. As he remembered the way she looked standing there in the steam, her come-hither smile driving him crazy with lust and desire, his breath would catch and his heart would skip a beat, as if just realizing that it was still beating. How was he still alive when his wife was gone? Never again able to experience any of life's joy, anger, or see their little girl grow up?

While it had been difficult for him to leave the home he and Heather had purchased in their second year of marriage, he knew it was for the best. There were good memories in that home, but he needed to be whole for his daughter. After he talked it over with both his parents and hers, he set out to find a house that represented renewal.

As soon as the realtor walked him through the front door of this house, he knew. This would be the place for them to have a new beginning. Taking deep breaths as he walked around, judging room sizes and picturing Madison growing up in this home, his decision had been made. Rebuild their lives, focus on work, and live a life focused on simply making it through each day.

"Mr. Branson, can you look over this order real quick?" The moving truck driver was standing a few feet away from him with a clipboard in his hand.

"Sure." As he grabbed the pen and clipboard, he heard vehicles pull up to the front of the house and looked up. His eyes glanced over at the house next to his and he saw the slightest movement in the window, as if someone were looking out. After a few seconds, he shrugged off the feeling of being watched. That type of thing was to be expected.

Everyone wanted to know what the new neighbors looked like and he couldn't fault them for that. Turning back to the cars pulling up to his new home, he ignored his nosey neighbor for the moment. His late wife's parents, Stan and Marge Tompkins, exited their car. His mother also had arrived right behind them. Lastly, his friends Rob and Leslie Morrison pulled up to the house, along with their little girl, and Madison's best friend, Bree. It was good to have all of them here.

After Heather's death, these were the people who had helped him continue to cope with the loss. They had stayed with him night and day. Every one of them had cooked and cleaned for him without complaint. In their own way, each of them had helped him understand that although Heather was gone from this world, he was not. It was Heather's father who had given him a swift kick in the rear, reminding him that he had lived through too much, come out on the other side of too much death and destruction in the military, to let her death beat him now. Chuckling under his breath at the old man's words, it was very clear that Stan Tompkins was not going to let his son-in-law wallow in self-pity.

Finishing his review of the work order, he signed his name and handed the clipboard back to the man standing in front of him. "Thanks, man. Everything looks in order. We'll try to stay out of the way as you and your guys get everything in the house."

"Appreciate that, we'll get the living room and dining room set up first so that you and your family have somewhere to sit," the driver responded. Tilting his head to the people walking toward them, the driver turned back to his crew and set them to work getting Cooper's furniture from the truck.

He gave Rob and Leslie a wave and went to grab Madison from the truck and placed her on the ground. As soon as she noticed Bree standing by her parent's car, she ran over and gave the little girl a tight hug. Shaking his head, he laughed at their antics. If he didn't know any better, he would think those two hadn't seen each other in years, instead of just yesterday at preschool. Walking over to the group of people, he gave greetings and hugs all around.

"Good to see you, Stan, Marge. I'm glad you could make it today."

"Son, we wouldn't have missed this for anything," his father-in-law responded.

Hearing the giggles of the two little girls talking animatedly with their hands, he put his hands in his pockets as he watched his mother walk over and give her granddaughter a kiss on the forehead.

Addressing his in-laws, he motioned toward the movers, "We're here a little earlier than expected, but these guys are going to get some of the basic furniture in the house for us first. We'll have somewhere to sit while they move the other items inside."

"No problem, Cooper," his mother-in-law answered. "Your mother and I brought some food for dinner, so we'll at least have food."

Motioning to Leslie, who was cuddled up close to her husband while smiling and looking toward the house, he asked, "Did you tell Leslie to bring a dish? You know she's a sous chef at that new restaurant in DC on 12th and 7th?"

Surprisingly, his mother-in-law waved his question away, "Oh, I'm sure she'll be fine. We don't need any help. She can watch the kids while your mother and I take care of the food."

Before he could question her about it, Leslie's voice caught his attention, "I swear, those two are like two peas in a pod. I don't know how in the world they have that much to talk about. It hasn't even been twenty-four hours since they saw each other last." She smiled at Cooper as she and her husband walked up to him. Leaning over, he kissed her on the temple.

"Oh, let them be. They're like BFF's or something. At least that's what I hear all the young kids are saying nowadays," he responded.

"Hey, man, she's taken," his friend Rob laughingly exclaimed as he pulled his wife closer to him.

Leslie laughed and kissed her husband lightly on the lips before turning back to greet Cooper's in-laws and his mother.

If Cooper was an envious man, he would admit that he missed having that type of relationship. Someone that was simply there for you. No judgement, just comfort and partnership.

As Leslie spoke to the grandparents, he caught Rob looking over at him. He raised his chin and then went in for a handshake and half-hug. "How are you doing, Coop? You all right?"

Without saying the words, Cooper knew what Rob was asking. Was he okay with the move, with giving up the house, basically, with moving on with his life?

"Yeah, man, I'm good." And as he said the words, he knew it was true. At that moment, both he and Rob turned toward the house next door. That feeling had come back again and he knew the house, or better yet, the person in that house, had something to do with it. Someone was there and they were watching.

Rob had been in Special Forces with Cooper and if he felt it, then so did his former Army brother. Leslie automatically turned to look as well. She had often picked up on their tendency to react to things at the same time. The running joke was that the two of them had gone through an experiment in the Army and their brains had been sliced in half, with each getting fifty-percent of the other's brain. If it weren't so wrong, he could actually believe it happened. There was no one he trusted more to have his back, to keep him sane, and to stand beside him than Rob Morrison.

It was the same house where he saw the woman peeking out of the window just a few minutes earlier. When Rob and Leslie turned away and began looking over the girls, laughing at their antics, Cooper continued to look at the window. Something kept his attention glued to that house and he wanted to know what, or who, it was.

It didn't feel like a threat. No, Rob would not have relaxed that soon if had been a threat to their families. But for some reason he couldn't look away just yet. He felt a soft hand on his arm and was forced to look away from the house. Looking down into the light blue eyes of his mother, he gave her a smile.

"Hi, Mom. Welcome to my home."

"Hi, honey. I'm so glad to be here. We all are. I see Madison and Bree haven't let go of each other since they stepped out of the cars." Laughing, she turned to him, "Did you buy that second bed for her?"

Laughing out loud, he grabbed her hand and tucked her arm over his as they walked toward the middle of the front yard where the others had gathered, "As if I could get away with not getting it. Do you remember the last time these two whirlwinds spent the night? Oh no, they're each having their own space."

Although he was drawn into the conversation and felt lighter than he had in months, something kept calling for his attention. As he motioned for everyone to go into the house, the need to look over and see if he could catch a glimpse of the woman looking at him through her front window took over. He glanced over just as she ducked out of the way. "Hmmm, interesting."

"What was that dear?" His mother-in-law looked over at him in curiosity.

"Oh nothing, just getting my bearings in the neighborhood."

Chapter Three

Listening to the sweet voice of his daughter as she and her best friend talked about everything that happened to them in the last twelve hours since they had been separated, he smiled. Walking into his new home, the start of the next chapter in his life, Cooper could appreciate that things had not turned out the way he had expected. Far from it.

A widower at thirty-eight was not his idea of a perfect life. Having his wife of twelve years die in a car crash six months after giving birth to their beautiful little girl had never been in the cards. It had taken him almost two years to get over the pain and hurt of losing Heather on that warm day in June.

He could still remember the moment he got the call from his boss and was asked to come to his office. Walking into the large corner office and seeing the two police officers waiting for him, he had no idea what to think. There would be no reason for the police to want to talk with him and he knew it, which only caused his confusion to grow. Never in a million years would he have expected their words to haunt him in his sleep for months, even years, after that meeting.

The officer who spoke first had a deep, raspy voice. "My name is Sergeant Isles from the Arlington County Police Department. Are you Cooper Branson, the husband of Heather Branson, of 321 Lee Boulevard?"

Looking toward my boss, I immediately noticed the look of sadness in his eyes before I turned back to the police and answered their questions, "What is this about?" My tone was a tad curter than the situation called for, but even in the few seconds I stood there, I knew it would be bad.

Just earlier that day, no more than three hours before, one of those gut feelings that something huge was about to happen had come over him. In that moment, he knew that his life would be changed forever. Having the cops show up at his office asking about his wife had not been on the list of possibilities.

Earlier that day, he had called Heather. Needing to speak with her after the feeling had come over him, they had been joking and laughing just minutes before she headed into a lunch meeting with a client.

"Baby, if you're pregnant, I want a boy this time."

"Who says I'm pregnant?" Her sweet voice responded with laughter. *"I'm not you know. But, even if I were, who says it's up to me what you get. Last I heard, it was the father who decided sex."*

Settling into his chair, he looked out the window as they continued to talk, *"Well, I just got that feeling and it usually happens when something huge is going to happen. Like when you were pregnant with Madison, and when I got this job offer, even when Rob and Leslie asked us to be the godparents for Bree."*

What he failed to mention, and never would, is that these feelings also came right before they were attacked by insurgents and the day his father had a heart attack. No, his focus that day was on the positives.

"I think you just want someone to watch football with." She laughed into the phone as he heard her turn off her car and exit.

"Nope, because Madison is going to be there, too. I'll make sure she gets the right kind of sports education." And no dating, he thought. There's no way in hell she'll date a boy like me.

Because of his career in the military, they had both agreed to wait until he had finished serving until they had children. Madison was born just six and a-half months ago at the time, and Heather had already been talking about having another one. Steeling his nerves for what he was about to hear, he spoke to the officer again, "Yes, I'm Cooper Branson. What can I do for you, Sergeant?"

The officer looked at him without blinking, as if schooling his features to deliver the next words out of his mouth, "Sir, I'm sorry to tell you, but there's been an accident."

Silence.

Although the police officer's mouth continued to move and words were coming out, Cooper didn't hear a word he said. The silence was deafening. Loud ringing was all he could hear and he tried to clear his head of the sound. What was the officer saying again? An accident? Dead on impact? It happened so quickly? She felt no pain? How do they know she didn't feel any pain? How do they know his wife didn't suffer for even one-second?

"Oh, God. This can't be happening," he managed to say the words, but hadn't really been aware of his actions. He then heard a keening wail that shattered his soul and it took a few seconds for him to realize it was coming from him. The sound was coming from inside of his soul and unbeknownst to him, had echoed across the entire 10th floor executive suite.

Heather had been his rock, the person who had gotten him through the difficult years of serving in the U.S. Army and the three tours in Iraq and Afghanistan. After all they had been through, and finally deciding to live their lives and raise a family, he was being told that someone had killed his wife at a stoplight in Alexandria, Virginia. She was never coming home again.

Blinking back to the present, Cooper knew that his gut feeling that day had been right. Only thing was, it hadn't been the stuff his dreams had been made of.

It had been the start of a nightmare.

Over time, he had learned to understand and interpret those feelings better and he knew that today, the feeling he had when looking over at his neighbor's house, had been new. Different. Unlike anything he had felt before. That scared him, but not in the way one would think.

It actually gave him hope. It meant there was a whole new experience in front of him. Life was throwing him a curveball. All he had to do was decide if he was going to strike out or swing for the fences. With one last look, he decided to just go with it and let life happen.

∞ ∞ ∞ ∞ ∞

Faith was nervous. She had spent the morning talking to herself like a loon and making up several reasons to not go and meet her new neighbors. Four casseroles later, three of which had already been thrown in the garbage after being deemed not good enough to serve to the dogs, so surely not good enough for her new neighbors. If she were thinking clearly, she would have remembered that she fully expected this man to be happily married. But for some reason, she couldn't stop the insane thoughts running through her head. Thinking clearly was not on the menu today.

So, here she stood. On her neighbor's doorstep, frozen in fear and with a healthy dose of embarrassment that she had dressed to impress a man who would probably have no interest in her.

"Damn, Denise, your fucking timing is impeccable." She knew those thoughts and insecurities were creeping in based on her ex-friend's cruel words, but she was determined to move forward. "Get it together, girl. Don't just stand out here staring at the damn door. Knock!"

Without waiting another second, she gave three strong raps on the front door. Her neighbor's truck was parked in the garage. She noticed it as she walked over. Maybe he saw her looking out her window yesterday and already decided that she wasn't worth getting to know in the first place. Especially if she had to gawk at people from the confines of her home. With no answer to her first knock, she decided to give up and try this another day.

Just as she started to turn around and head back home, she was hit with a sense of sadness. Not because there was no answer to her knock, but the one time she had forced herself do something brave, it hadn't worked.

Did she expect anything to come from taking a casserole to her neighbor? No, not really. But the sadness was still there, no doubt stemming from the questions she had asked herself many times over during these past few days.

Mainly, would there ever be a man who would stimulate both her mind and her body at the same time? Someone that she wanted, someone she chose, and not just the guy who wanted to pursue her for the sake of experiencing what it was like to sleep with a thick girl.

Her sexual drought wasn't because there hadn't been opportunities for her, or because men had no interest in her. It was that she hadn't yet met the one man who made her want more than just sex.

That was until she saw her neighbor standing on the front lawn of his new home in jeans and a t-shirt, laughing at the antics of two little girls and treating women in his life, old and young, with respect and care.

As she took her first step toward freedom—and her empty home—she heard the door swing open behind her. For just a smidgen of a second, she almost kept going. This was so stupid. It was probably his wife and Faith would look like a fool.

Regret began to spread through her like a wildfire, and then she turned around. As she came face-to-face with the man standing in front her, covered in sweat and dust from no doubt getting his home in order, her inner diva finally chose to show up to the party. Throwing caution to wind, she leapt into the storm and prayed she would come out alive and whole on the other side.

Finding her voice, she pushed the casserole dish in his direction. Forcing him to grab the warm dish with both hands, "Hi. I'm your next door neighbor, Faith Douglas."

"Um, hello, Faith, I'm Cooper Branson."

"I'm Madison!"

Looking down, she noticed his daughter peeking through his arm and the door. Wide, blue eyes staring up at the strange lady standing at their door. Leaning over so that she was on closer eye-level with the curious child, she held out her hand to shake, "It's very nice to meet you, little Madison. Welcome to the neighborhood." Surprised when she stuck out her little hand to grab Faith's, she gave it two quick up-and-down motions. Giving her a smile, she was already enamored with the precocious child. Faith released her tiny hand and stood back up to take in the up-close and personal view of her father.

The smile on his face was something to behold. And he had dimples. Well, damn. 'Could this man get any fucking better?' was the first thought that floated through her mind. Still, she hadn't seen the wife, but that didn't mean she wasn't around somewhere.

Within moments of that thought, her neighbor must have thought of something that changed his entire mood. His eyebrows turned down and his brow furrowed in a look of annoyance. Looking at both Madison and Faith, he was not happy about something. Uh oh, had she stepped over some pre-determined line?

"Well, I just wanted to let you know that I live in next house over. I'm very close in case you need anything." Okay…this was not turning out the way she expected. "Is your wife home?"

"I don't have a wife."

Elation spread through her at his words.

"My mommy died when I was a baby," she heard the little girl say as she entered he conversation.

Well, shit. Dread stomped on that elation, jumping up and down on it like it was a bug in a pristine kitchen.

She looked at her neighbor with a touch of sadness, shock, and true awe. He was a tall, sexy, widower raising a precocious little girl. If it weren't so sad, it would be the stuff of romance novels.

His only response to his daughter's statement was to continue looking at her with his piercing ice blue gaze, never taking his eyes from her face. Not even for a second.

Adjusting his position and placing the casserole dish on a side table sitting next to the door, he lifted one hand to leisurely rest one his lean hip, a slight smile tilting his lips on one side. "Well, with that cheery opening, thank you for the casserole, Mrs. Douglas."

"Well, I know what it's likc to move into a new home and have to unpack and then get all of your food unpacked. Then if you don't want to order pizza, the only other choices aren't very good. So, I figured I would do something nice for you and your family. I'm sorry...I didn't know you weren't married. I just thought your wife wasn't with you when you moved in yesterday…"

Trailing off, her eyes began to nervously drift away from his face. Her gaze soon landed on his chest and arms, his white t-shirt was form-fitting and fit his toned form perfectly. Unable to stop her eyes from shifting downward, she stopped briefly at the unmistakable bulge in his well-worn jeans. Positive that her mouth dropped open just a fraction, the clear and distinct outline of his package was very visible.

The way his jeans fit his lower torso, riding low on his hips made her think some very naughty, dirty, "not to be discussed in the daytime" thoughts about her new neighbor. Getting this far, there was no way in hell she was stopping now. Go big or go home was her new motto, so she was taking this to the endgame.

Glancing down at his feet, she guessed that he must have worn size thirteen, easily. With that realization, she must have made a noise as the limitless possibilities began to run through her mind. Just as she was starting to forget why she was even standing here, her new neighbor, whom she had known for all of two minutes, cleared his throat. Quickly lifting her gaze back up to his face, she felt her face turn hot in embarrassment. To be caught openly ogling the man while he stood in his front door was so inappropriate. This was totally not like her.

Tilting his head, his eyes crinkled up at her and his nose flared out. Not in anger, but maybe in frustration and annoyance. Maybe he was used to this and women undressed him in public all the time.

"Find something interesting, Mrs. Douglas?" Damn, now that was distinctly unfriendly. Although her skin had a beautiful pecan hue, she was positive the red flush of embarrassment and mortification was coming through quite clearly.

Could it be called sexual harassment if she was only enjoying the scenery? Okay, fine! She was way out of line and if a man had done the same thing to her, she would be downright pissed right now.

Knowing she was the one in the wrong, she nodded her head once, acknowledging her error. Forcing her eyes back to his face, she realized this actually didn't help very much at all. He was just yummy goodness from his head to his toes.

"It's Ms."

"Excuse me?" His voice had not softened one bit and that's when she realized that this must be his normal tone of voice.

Two seconds later, some pesky butterflies took up residence in her stomach.

Finding her voice again, she continued, "I was just saying that I'm a Ms. I'm not married. Not that it matters or anything. I mean, it would matter. Because if I were married, my husband would be here with me and I never would have looked at you like you were a popsicle on a hot summer day."

Her eyes widened and her brain began to short-circuit. Oh My God! "I mean...hell, you know what I mean. I'm sorry." Looking behind her, she wanted to crawl into a hole and hide her head like an ostrich. "How about we start over. I'll take my casserole back to the house, take my foot out of my mouth, wait five minutes and try it again."

After a few seconds, a burst of laughter came out of his mouth. She watched a change come over him and he seemed to transform into another person right in front of her eyes. If she thought he was sexy before, that was nothing compared to seeing him with a smile on his face and his eyes crinkled up in laughter. Opening the door wider, the smile remained on his face as he motioned for her to come in.

"Don't worry about it, Ms. Douglas. Come on in. I'm pretty much done for the day and your dish will come in handy." Stepping to the side, he allowed her space to step through the door and into his home.

"Faith." She said as she moved further into his home.

"Excuse me? I didn't catch that." Clicking the door closed, he picked up the dish from the table he had placed it on earlier, and turned toward the back of the house. As he began walking in the direction of the kitchen, she turned in the same direction and began following him.

Bad move. She caught her first glimpse of his powerful, confident walk, and it just completed the whole picture. If she weren't such a good girl, and his daughter wasn't peeking around corners trying to take in the scene, she would climb his fine ass like a tree in the jungle and change her name to Jane.

"Ms. Douglas, are you distracted again?"

Looking up at the back of his head, she wondered how the hell he knew she was looking at his firm behind and drooling over thoughts about the motion in his ocean. "Huh? Say what?"

Stopping to turn around and look at her, he had a smirk on his face, "That's what I asked you. You said something and then went silent on me."

Thinking quickly, she tried to recall what the hell they were talking about. Oh, her name! The man had made her forget her own name and they weren't even naked and rolling around on the floor doing naughty, adult things to each other? Now that was a feat. "Faith. Please, call me Faith."

Smiling slyly at her after she finished her statement, she could tell that he knew exactly what had happened and why. Oh yes, she thought, he's dangerous. Then again, maybe this was what she needed. Just some good old-fashioned fun.

"Okay. Faith it is. Then you'll have to call me Cooper, and this one," turning toward his daughter and pointing with his elbow, "of course, is Madison. Although my little social butterfly already introduced herself, which I will address with her later." Glancing over at his daughter, he watched her as she slowly walked into the large open kitchen and mini dining area.

"Great. Cooper and Madison it is," she responded.

Tilting his chin toward the stools situated on one side of the kitchen breakfast bar, he turned toward the stove, "Go on. Have a seat. Let me take a look at what you brought over for us." As he proceeded to lift the lid and take in the smell of the pasta dish she had stressed over this morning, Faith felt a tug on her arm.

"Hi, little munchkin," she greeted the blonde-haired little girl.

"Hi, Ms. Faith. I want to sit next to you. Help me." Lifting her arms in the air, she allowed Faith to lift her and place on her on the seat right next to her. Cooper looked back at them, a curious glance on his face as he watched his daughter interact with her.

"Well, then I guess that makes it official. You brought us food, which smells delicious by the way, you ogled my body…"

Dropping her head into her hands, "I'm really sorry about that." His laughter broke into her apology.

"Really, it's okay." Grabbing a towel to wipe his hands, he looked at Faith. "So, now that the official miniature welcoming committee has accepted you into our abode, I think we're all settled. Would you agree?"

Looking down at Madison, she shrugged her shoulders, "What do you think, Madison? Are we ready?"

"Yes!"

Grabbing plates out of the cabinet and placing the casserole in the oven, he turned back to the two of them. "So, what do we want to do now?"

Madison raised her hand in the air and at the same time yelled out, "I know! I know!"

Her father pointed at her, "Okay, Madison, what would you like to do?"

Looking at Faith with a smile filled with little white teeth tinted with red from her fruit juice, she asked, "Do you like princess movies?"

Chapter Four

Waking up to the bright sun coming through his bedroom window, Cooper yawned and stretched out on his king size bed. Picking up his phone, he read the messages from Faith that had come through last night and gave a sigh of relief.

It had only taken a few weeks after that initial meeting, and several instances of her coming to them first, before he and Madison changed things up. Pretty soon, they were the ones showing up at her door instead. After all, he was just being neighborly.

At least, that was the story he continued to tell himself as he tried to understand why he couldn't stay away from her.

Cooper wondered how different his life would be if he and Madison had never met their lovely neighbor. After that first day of bringing them food and staying for hours as they got to know each other, even helping to put away some of their unpacked items, they had built a routine. Every weekend after that, there she was, at their door with food. It was like she was always feeding them, making sure they ate something new and different every time. Asking them what they liked, preferred, and absolutely hated.

He wasn't sure when the weekends, and seeing Faith, had become so important to him. But it had. Over the past two months, his need to be around Faith had grown as much as his daughter's. He was most relaxed when in her presence, even when doing the most mundane tasks. Whatever it was that was happening, he was willing to let it just ride. There was no need to rush anything and he wouldn't.

Something about Faith continued to draw him closer to her whenever they came in contact with each other. Not sure what it was about her that kept him thinking about her at the most inopportune times, like when he was sitting in the middle of an operations meeting. Someone mentioned the word faith and he had immediately pictured her smiling face.

Honestly, he wasn't ready to consider the possibilities as to why she never failed to be far from his thoughts. He would tackle that puzzle another day. As for right now, he was just focused on enjoying the moment.

If only he could allow himself to let her in. Not many people knew the real him and it was hard to share that side of him with anyone. Every day he struggled with the demons that tried to tear him down. His time in the Army and serving overseas, the casualties of war by his own hands, and the death of his wife that still sometimes haunted him in his dreams.

The kid with anger issues had found his way into the military through a stroke of luck, or maybe it had been fate. Either way, it made him into a different man. Life in the military had been mostly good, but other times, not so much. After his marriage to Heather, and raising his beautiful little girl all alone, he had become a different man. It had taken him a while to get there, but Cooper knew that he was now comfortable in this new, buttoned up world around him. And he was okay with that.

However, Faith Douglas had come into his world and she had thrown him for a loop. She was almost the exact opposite of the type of women he normally would be interested in dating. If anyone had asked him a year ago to describe his ideal woman, he probably would have described his late wife. Now, after meeting Faith, he wasn't so sure.

But based on her reaction to him over these past couple of months, it seemed that she considered him as only a friend. Not once had she ever given any indication that she wanted anything more than their friendly, flirty banter. That was part of the reason why it bothered him so much that just seeing her face would make him want to be around her, talk with her, and hear her voice even more.

Even his daughter was drawn to the nice lady who had brought them into her world from the very first day they moved into the neighborhood. It seemed that Madison had decided that there was only one speed when it came to Faith. Full steam ahead.

There was no stopping Madison when she wanted something. Within a week of meeting her, all she wanted was Faith. And when his little girl wanted to see Faith that was all that mattered. No longer willing to wait for Faith to come to them, she would wake up on the weekends and within minutes, would ask to go see the lovely Ms. Faith.

Telling himself that he was doing it for Madison, he would usually give in and they would head over to spend the day. As time passed, he began to notice that he was also starting to become excited at the thought of spending time with her. Each time he woke up on the weekends, he would lie there and countdown the minutes until Madison would come ask to call Faith and plan their day.

Her number was programmed into his phone, number three on the speed-dial list. He never failed to call and let her know that they were on their way over, just in case she had other plans. But never once had she said no or denied them. Which, if he had taken a moment to truly think about, would have told him more than he would have imagined.

Seeing her every weekend had become like second nature. It was just something that he had to do. Felt he needed to do. And today was no different.

This morning, waking up from a restless sleep, he wondered where Faith had been last night. After several calls to her cell phone with no answer, he had texted her asking where she was. There had been an uneasy feeling rolling around his stomach and he wasn't happy at all that she hadn't been picking up. When she finally did respond, his frustration had only grown. And then he got pissed off, because he wasn't supposed to feel that way about her.

Picking up his phone again to look at the text messages from last night, he felt his back teeth begin to grind in frustration.

9:15pm, Hey Faith, you working late?

9:18pm, Faith, you're not picking up. Everything okay?

9:22pm, Hi Cooper. Yes, I'm fine. I'll be home a little late.

9:23pm, You're safe? At the office? Faith, you can't do that to me.

9:27pm, Sorry. Definitely safe. Tell Madison I'll talk to her tomorrow. Nite.

Her messages had been vague and that had actually pissed him off even more. Where had she been? Not that she had to clear her schedule with him, but they had somewhat of a routine. They spoke every night without fail. It wasn't like Faith to simply ignore him and not call or let him know where she was. The last message had come through at almost midnight.

11:52pm, Hey Cooper, just letting you know I made it home safe. Talk later.

Rolling out of bed, he pulled on some pajama pants and a t-shirt before walking downstairs. Fulling expecting Madison to get in her request for them to see Faith as soon as she came downstairs, he pre-empted her and called before she came asking.

"Hello?" Her sleep tinged voice filled the line.

"Hi, Faith, it's me, Cooper," he said. Again, he wondered where she had been last night. The only thought he could come up with was that she went out with some friends from work. But why wouldn't she just say that?

Sounds of her moving around in bed came across the phone and he wondered what she slept in. Was she the type to sleep in negligee or a nightshirt? If he showed up one morning without his customary call, how would she answer the door? Would her lips be full and pouty, her long, thick hair messy, as if she had just rolled out of bed?

"Hi, Cooper." The rustling covers that could be heard made his body begin to respond to the picture that formed in his head. What the hell was that all about?

Clearing his throat to make sure he didn't come off too gruff, "Madison and I were wondering if we could come over and make you lunch today."

"Oh, you were? Um, why?"

Laughing at her surprise, he knew she was a keeper. Wait, a keeper for what? He wasn't looking for a keeper of anything. Turning back to the conversation at hand and ignoring those wayward thoughts, "Well, because you always cook for us, or pick up something while you're out. I thought we would return the favor."

Feeling a tug on his shirt, he looked down to see Madison standing there in her superhero pajamas, her tiny feet straining as she stood on her toes. Her hands were folded together as if in prayer. A wide smile spread across her face, "We're going to make you a dad-burger, Ms. Faith," she yelled out.

Turning his attention back to the phone again, "Did you hear that?"

"I sure did," she answered. "It's nine o'clock now. What time will you be here?"

"How about eleven-thirty?" Thinking about the items he already had, he knew a trip to the store would be in order.

"Okay, that sounds good. I'll be ready." A yawn came through the phone. "Um, but what is a dad-burger?" She asked.

The huskiness of her voice continued to pull at him. Then again, he wondered why she was still asleep at this hour. Ignoring her question about the food, he asked his own, "You sound tired. Long week?"

"Yes, work's been tough, but I can handle it," she said.

"Okay, just want to make sure you're not pushing yourself too hard. Those people don't know just how good you are." Maybe it wasn't his place to tell her to rest, but he didn't care about that. She was his friend and he was worried she was pushing herself too hard. "Make sure they understand just how much you do for them. Working late on a—"

"I had a date last night," she interjected.

His breath left his body for a few seconds. Did he hear her right? "A date?"

"Yeah. Um, a lady at work set me up with her husband's friend and we met for dinner last night," she said. Her voice was somewhat low and hesitant as she shared this with him.

"I don't…Wait a minute. Who were you with? Are you going to see him again," he demanded to know. So, is this the reason why she hadn't told him where she was last night?

"Cooper, why does it matter?"

There was no anger in her tone. He, on the other hand, was building to a slow boil. Fuck! A date? Why hadn't she told him?

"Anyway, as I said, what's a dad-burger?"

Asking her question again, he knew she was trying to get him off topic, which was probably a good thing. His reaction to her saying that she had a date last night didn't make any sense to him.

"Well, a dad-burger is my very own recipe for making burgers on the grill. My recipe is so secret, only those in my special circle know the ingredients. Even then, they only know what I use, but not how much goes into the mixture," he finally answered.

"Are you going to tell me? Am I in your special circle?"

If only she knew. "Do you want to be?"

"It depends, what do I have to do?" This time, the huskiness in her voice sounded different to his ears. Sleep was not the cause.

"Whatever I want," he responded. They were getting into dangerous territory, but he liked the way things were going. Plus, if there was another man sniffing around, he needed to change that…quickly.

Although he hadn't officially staked his claim, there was no one else good enough for Faith but him. He dared a motherfucker to try and step in and claim the woman he was quickly coming to realize meant more to him than he thought.

"Oh, really," she laughingly exclaimed. "That sounds ominous."

"Nah, once you're in the special circle of trust, you'll never want to leave," he said. By now, he was sitting in a chair and Madison had left the room, probably bored that the conversation wasn't centered on her.

"Oh...is that right?"

"Trust me," he said as he stood and walked over to the foyer and stood in front of the stairs. "We'll be there at eleven-thirty. I have to run some errands first. It's my in-laws anniversary next week and I need to pick up a gift for them."

"Oh, do you need any help," she asked.

Pleased by her willingness to lend a hand, he was tempted to accept her offer to come along, but decided against it. "No, but thanks. I feel close to Heather when I do stuff for her parents. I know she's there with me, helping me to pick out what's best. It feels good to still be able to have that connection with her. It helps me to not forget what we had."

Not noticing the silence on the other end of the line as he began walking up the stairs to shower, get dressed, and leave the house, he continued, "Okay, so we'll see you in a few, okay?"

"Um, sure Cooper. I'll be here. Bye."

Cooper was a smart man. But like every man, he sometimes failed to look beyond his own needs and feelings. All he knew was that he now desired his neighbor. More than that, he wanted her for his own. Selfish though it may be, considering he still slept with a picture of his late wife next to his bed.

That didn't matter to him. All he cared about were his feelings right now. And what he felt was that it would be a cold day in hell before he gave her up without a fight.

However, what he failed to realize was that he wasn't free to belong to anyone. At least not yet. Having no clue as to why Faith's voice had dropped an octave and the happiness he heard just a few minutes ago was no longer there, he ended the call.

"Bye, sugar. See you later."

Chapter Five

Cooper took in the scene in front of him and couldn't help but feel good. The three of them sat in Faith's dining room a few weeks later, their dinner plates full of food cooked by Faith. For some reason, the woman had gotten it into her head that he and Madison needed to eat Brussels sprouts.

It had taken her weeks of pleading and convincing to get him to even agree that she could make them for dinner one night. His nose wrinkled up as he leaned over his plate and took a whiff. For such little things, the smell was horrible and it permeated throughout the entire house.

There had been no way in hell he would agree to her making them in his kitchen. Even now, he still wasn't sure how she managed to get his agreement that he would even eat the things. But, after all was said and done, he had made a deal. If she cooked them in her own kitchen, in her own home, then he would at least give them a try.

After all of her arguments and research on the healthy impact of eating a variety of leafy, green vegetables—which she fully considered Brussels sprouts to be—he hadn't the heart to tell her he abhorred the things. If given a choice, he would rather go to the ballet than eat the crunchy, almost deformed looking, miniature cabbages.

As a result, he was committed to suffering in silence because he hadn't wanted to disappoint her. It was his own damn fault.

Smiling brightly, Faith had sat in front of him as he speared his first sprout and lifted the fork to his mouth. Looking over at Madison, he gave her a wink as the little girl giggled. Wearing a smug look of satisfaction on her face, she stared at him intently. He knew she was waiting to gauge his reaction. Faith's eyes never wavered, but he noticed that she was biting and nibbling on her bottom lip. He exhaled deeply. Why had he never noticed how sexy it was when she did that?

She had even stopped eating her own meal as she waited. Watching him closely as he took his first bite and chewed slowly, she leaned forward, anticipating his response.

"You love them, right?" Her question came just as he was mid-chew. Beaming with pride the entire time, she began eating her own food while he forced himself to continue chewing and not spit the offending food from his mouth.

On the other hand, if the speed of her fork entering her mouth was any indication, Madison seemed to love the things. Unfortunately for him, he knew it was simply too late for his taste buds to change.

Chewing quickly, he tried to get it down his throat as fast as he could without actually tasting the vegetable. Forcing himself to swallow the entirety of the offending piece of food, he briefly closed his eyes as his stomach fought the urge to rebel in horror. Taking a quick drink, he tried not to look like a recalcitrant child as he answered, "They're good. I've never really tasted any like yours before. You definitely have a unique touch."

Hoping she hadn't seen through him to recognize the lie that had passed his lips, he quickly moved on to eating his grilled pork chops as if they were the best thing created out of a kitchen since...well, anything ever.

"I knew you would like them," she stated in triumph as she took another bite of her own food.

"I like them, Ms. Faith," exclaimed Madison as she entered the conversation.

"I'm glad you do, sweetheart," Faith responded as she held up her hand for Madison to give her a high five.

Watching the two of them in action, he would swear that his little girl would claim to love anything Faith gave to her. Her growing affection for their lovely neighbor made him smile. He could also completely understand it, since he felt a growing affection for her as well. And day by day, it was becoming harder to ignore.

∞ ∞ ∞ ∞ ∞

Opening the door at the sound of the doorbell, Faith admired the sight in front of her. Dressed casually in light brown shorts and a blue shirt, Cooper looked completely different than he did during the week. Faith liked what she saw.

"Hey, you two! I'm almost ready," she said as she picked up her purse and a large blanket that she used for sitting on the grass.

"Come on, Faith! This is going to be so much fun!" Madison was giddy with excitement.

They were headed to the National Mall in the heart of Washington, DC. Today there was a huge kite event and they were joining the fun. People from all over would come and fly huge, colorful, and intricate kites all day long. It was a sight to see and Faith had been to the event a few times. Today was the first time she would see it through the eyes of a child.

"Alright, I'm ready!" Locking the door behind her, they all packed into Cooper's truck and made their way into the city.

It was hard for the two of them to get a word in edgewise over the chatter of Madison's voice. "I want to fly a big kite and then I want to run really fast and it's gonna fly in the sky really high." Her voice carried throughout the vehicle.

"Thanks for inviting us today," Cooper glanced over at Faith briefly. Reaching out for her hand, he gave a squeeze.

Looking at their joined hands, her heart skipped a beat and her stomach started to flutter with nervousness and a bit of anticipation. Tempted to hold on to his hand a little longer, to maintain their connection, she placed her other hand on top of his.

"You're welcome, Cooper. I think you two will have a great time." Glancing back at Madison who had fallen silent for all of three minutes, "Madison will love it. It's very exciting, even for me. I can only imagine what she'll think."

Coming to a turn, Cooper glanced down and smiled at their hands. Feeling a slight pull of his hand, she released him and placed her hands on her legs. Although she was tempted to be embarrassed, she quelled the feeling. For all he knew, it was a friendly overture. How would he know that even a brief connection, whether it was grabbing the other's hands, or a kiss on the cheek or forehead as they parted, drew her even closer to him.

"Park over there by the World War II Memorial. The walk will do us good," she told him, pointing in the direction of the memorial site.

"I don't come into D.C. very often anymore. Heather and I used to come here for dinner quite often, or to the theatre," Cooper said with ease.

She wasn't even sure if he realized how casually he spoke about his wife in her presence. Noting that he did this quite often, she held her tongue, not quite knowing how to respond to what he said. A few minutes of silence filled the vehicle as he found a parking spot and parallel parked.

As soon as the vehicle stopped and the engine was turned off Madison began chatting away, "Faith, will the kites be really big?" In her excitement, Madison was unbuckling herself from her car seat without waiting for one of them to help.

"Hold on, princess. Let your dad help you. This is a very busy area," she cautioned the little girl. All she needed was for something to happen on the one day that Cooper had agreed to spend the day outside of their neighborhood.

For the past few months, as they got settled into their new home, Cooper and Madison had been getting to know Faith. And Faith had been falling in love with Cooper. She had known it for weeks now, maybe even the last two months. Refusing to admit how she felt, she tried her best to keep her feelings hidden.

"Hey, Faith, are you ready?" His deep voice echoed throughout the vehicle. She was still sitting in her seat, buckled in, while they were both outside of the car. Cooper's light blue eyes gave her a questioning look as he noticed that she had not moved.

Figuring that she would take advantage of the day given to her, she put a smile on her face and got out of the truck. Today was not a day to focus on the 'what ifs' and dissect her feelings for the sexy single father. It was all about fun, food, and flying kites today.

"I know the perfect spot for our picnic," she announced.

Madison let go of her father's hand and grabbed onto hers, "Faith, can I walk with you? Daddy has his hands full with our stuff."

Glancing over her shoulder, she noticed that Cooper did indeed have his hands full. Blanket, picnic basket full of food that he had prepared for them, a brand new kite for them to open, and a big goofy smile on his face to complete the picture.

"Are you sure you can handle all that," she laughingly asked.

Shrugging his shoulders, he looked at the stuff around him. "Of course, I can. Do you know, when I was in the Army, I could pack eighty pounds of gear into rucksack the size of Madison's book bag? This is nothing," he noted with a smirk. He turned on his heel and started walking toward the intersection in the direction of the Washington Monument.

"Okay, okay, Mr. I Can Pack Anything into a Thimble." Looking down at Madison, she laughed out loud when the little girl starting shaking her head.

"Daddy, you always say that!"

Yup, she was one smart, sassy little girl. Faith loved it!

∞ ∞ ∞ ∞ ∞

"Wow, I am worn out," Faith flopped down on Cooper's couch and laid her head on the back.

"Yeah, you and me both." Cooper had just returned from putting Madison down for a nap.

The day trip had been a resounding success. The kites were big and beautiful and they were entertained for hours. Madison had run from one end of the mall to the other, oohing and ahhing over everything in her sight.

Faith pulled one foot underneath her as she turned her body in his direction. Staring at him for a few minutes, she admired his chiseled profile as he sat just feet away from her, his eyes closed. "She loved her kite, Cooper. Where did you find a princess picture that looked exactly like her?"

Opening his eyes, he caught her staring and she pulled her eyes away, looking at her hands. As he started to speak, she looked over at him again, free to admire him without feeling self-conscious.

"There's this little novelty shop I found in Reston. One day I stopped by the place just to waste some time while waiting for a wom—for a friend," he said.

Noticing his slip and correction, she wondered what that was all about. She knew he dated. He had never hid the fact that he was trying to reclaim some of his life again. They had never discussed it, but she knew. She just tried to not let it bother her. Not too much, anyway.

"But how does the kite look just like Madison," she asked.

"Well, they will create anything you want with any material you want. All I had to do was provide them a small picture of Madison and they created a kite that had her face on it. It cost a small fortune, but it was worth it to see her face today," he smiled as any proud father would after doing something amazing for their child.

They fell into a comfortable silence as they both took deep breaths. It felt good to relax after a long day out in the sun.

"Thirsty?" Cooper's voice broke into her thoughts.

Lifting her head for a just a second, "Oh, goodness, yes! Do you have any iced tea?"

"Of course I do. I know you too well now. I always have iced tea waiting for you." Getting up from the couch, he toed off his shoes and walked barefoot into the kitchen.

Basking in the feeling of just being here with him like this, she wondered what would happen if she let it be known that she wanted more. Would he push her away? Did he have any idea just how much she sometimes wanted to run her hands through his short hair? Her fingers itched to touch his cheek or skim across his chest. To feel his warm skin underneath her palms.

This felt good, being with him—with Madison—like this. Uncertainty and fear was holding her back, though. He hadn't given any indication that he wanted more and she was not willing to risk what they had.

Although Cooper rarely talked about what happened to his wife, he did share the basics. She knew he loved his wife more than his own life. Even though she tried not to, she couldn't help but wonder how much of Madison's personality was her own, and how much she had received from each of her parents. Cooper seemed so laid back most of the time, but there were moments—dark moments when there was a lingering sadness reflected in his eyes. Knowing what she did about his backstory, it was either memories of his time in the Army or the memories of his life with Heather. Neither one boded well, but only one made her question what she was doing here with him. With a man who continued to hold on to the past.

Initially, he had been very closed off and it had taken her quite a bit of effort to get him to open up to her. It wasn't as if he really had a choice. After seeing the two of them move in, it quickly became clear that it was only the two of them and she had appointed herself as their welcoming committee. Her mind had jumped to the idea that a divorce had been involved until after that first meeting when the true reason there was no wife or mother included in their little family was shared with her. The full story as to what happened to Heather had taken quite a while to get out of Cooper.

Looking back, she smiled at the memory of their first meeting. She had been a goner from the beginning and there had been no stopping that train from leaving the station. Her world had shifted and her brain and heart had finally come into alignment. Before him, there had been other opportunities, other men who were either attractive or stimulating, but never both. Had she been tempted to throw caution to the wind? Of course. She had been tempted many, many times.

But with this man, in this moment, she could admit that no one had ever made her feel this way. Every moment she spent with him was better than the last. Never in her adult life had she craved a man as much as she craved Cooper. It felt as if she needed him in her life. She breathed easier when she was near him.

Hearing him come back from the kitchen, she held out her hand for her drink. With his own cold drink in hand, Cooper sat back down next to her on the couch. Giving her a side glance, he closed one eye, giving her a wink as he took a long swallow.

"So, how's work? Everything going okay? You mentioned some new work coming in that might have you traveling to Denver," he asked.

He remembered her talking about that from weeks ago? Setting her own glass on the side table, she crossed one leg over the other, "Yes, I think I'll have to go there in the next few weeks."

Motioning to her to give him one of her feet, "Rest your feet on me. You did as much walking as I did today."

"No, Cooper, you don't have to do that," she demurred. Although, a foot massage would feel really good right now.

"Come on, lift them up. I want to." Grabbing one leg, which set her body tingling at the first touch, he lifted one leg, then the other, over his lap.

"Okay, if you insist." One denial was enough. If he wanted to give her a foot massage, then who was she to deny him the pleasure. And herself. "Thanks, Cooper."

His hands began kneading the arch of her left foot and she almost had an orgasm. Oh, fuck! That feels so good. The man had very strong hands, which she knew, but she had never felt a massage like this. She was religious about getting a pedicure every other week and a foot massage came with the service. But never in her life had she felt something this good. He knew just the right amount of pressure to apply and when to release. Thumbs and fingers worked in tandem, loosening the tendons in her foot. “Mmmmm, that feels so damn good.”

Was that her voice? It sounded like she was in the middle of some good loving. Hell, she felt as if she were being made love to. Eyes closed in bliss, she wasn’t aware that she had continued to moan out her pleasure at the sensation until Cooper called her name.

“Faith.”

Another moan.

“Faith! Sweetheart, are you even listening to me?” He laughed and that got her attention, “Fuck, woman, if this is what you sound like when getting a foot massage, I wonder how you sound in bed.”

Faith’s eyes shot open and her head popped up in alarm. Oh, shit!

∞ ∞ ∞ ∞ ∞

His ears heard the sounds coming from Faith’s mouth, but he didn’t think she realized what she was doing. Peeking up from under his lashes at the woman sitting on his couch in a trance-like state, he almost lost it. Her head was tilted back on the couch, her eyes were closed, and the moans echoing across the room made his dick rock hard.

Whoa! Put on the brakes! Faith was his friend. When did he start thinking of her that way? When? Hell, the moment she started making sounds of ecstasy sitting next to him while his hands were on her body. That's when.

"Fuck, woman. If this is what you sound like when getting a foot massage, I wonder how you sound in bed," the words were said before he could pull them back. Images of the two of them in bed entered his mind. He couldn't help but picture her in the throes of passion, making sounds just like this as he stroked in and out of her. Suddenly, his fingers itched to touch her bare skin. His lips tingled with the thought of suckling on her hard nipples and feeling her hands wrap around his shoulders. Just as he was getting deeper into his fantasy, Faith jumped up and tried to pull away from him.

"Don't be embarrassed, Faith. It must have felt good." Feeling her pull her feet off of his lap, he protested, "No, don't move. I like this. I like knowing that I can do something to make you happy."

Dropping her head in her hands, she seemed to gather herself and then looked at him again, "Fine, but no more commenting on how I sound in bed."

Picking up the motion with his hands again, he questioned, "Why not?"

"Because you're not supposed to know, or care, what I sound like in bed," she quipped back. Crossing her arms over her ample chest, as if to close herself off from him, she gave him a stern look.

His eyes were drawn to the movement, he watched her breasts adjust and move as her arms folded under them. Unbidden, another rolling scene that featured him and Faith naked and entwined on the floor of his family room popped into his head.

Vivid pictures played in his mind and he simply allowed them to play. He wanted to understand just how far he was willing to take this. His mouth watered as he continued to think about how it would feel to be latched onto one of her breasts, suckling on one of her nipples as he thrust his cock into her hot channel. How would it feel to have her thick legs wrapped around his waist, locking him in tight to her body? Not allowing him to pull away from her as she took her pleasure from his body. Her screams and moans of ecstasy the only sound in the room as he claimed her…claimed the woman that made him finally want more.

"Cooper."

Feeling a nudge on his arm, he looked up at Faith. Something on his face must have reflected his inner thoughts. Because she gasped as she looked at him, her eyes widening first in alarm, then in something else. If she didn't know better, she would think he was feeling and thinking the same thing.

"Cooper, I should go now," she whispered to him.

It took a few moments for him to answer, "Why?"

Shifting to sit up, her feet slowly moved away from his lap, which he allowed this time. Faith reached down and grabbed her shoes from where she had placed them when they arrived to the house. "It's late. We've had a long day. We're both tired." Standing up, she began to gather her other belongings, looking around the room as if she were missing something.

Lifting up from the couch, he came to stand in front of her. Just inches separated their bodies, but it felt like miles. Now that the thought had entered his head, he couldn't—wouldn't—allow it to just leave. He watched her fidget and knew she was nervous.

"You okay, Faith? You can stay. We can eat something," he said as he closed the distance between them.

She stood there, not moving as he brought his body flush with hers. Everything in him wanted to just rip her clothes off and take what he wanted, but he knew that wasn't the move he needed to make. Faith needed time. Maybe she needed to catch up with where hc was.

"I'm fine, Cooper," she responded breathlessly.

"Alright. If you say so," he said while stepping back from her. Giving her the space to leave, he simply watched as she stayed in her place. Her eyes held confusion and uncertainty as she looked from him to the door.

Oh, sweetheart, all you have to do is make a choice, he thought to himself. Out loud, he said, "Change your mind?"

Jumping at the sound of his voice, she quickly started to move toward the door, "No, I'm good. Okay, I'll see you later. Maybe tomorrow." She opened the door, backing out as she continue to speak. "It was fun today, but I'm just so tired."

"I understand," he said as he continued stalking toward her. In five seconds, if she wasn't already gone, she would be staying the night with him and his cock would be balls deep inside of her within ten minutes. Silently, he started to count. One...Two...forcing her to accept him wasn't in the cards. Three... but he would do everything in his power to make her beg for it...Four…

"Okay, night, Cooper," she closed the door just as he got to the count of five.

Torn between allowing her to walk out the door and not allowing her to leave his sight and carrying her caveman style upstairs to his bedroom, Cooper tried to calm down his heated libido. If he thought about it, could he even explain to himself why his feelings for Faith were all jumbled up in his brain all of a sudden? Well, maybe not all of a sudden. Things had been changing between them for a while, but he was now ready to give it a name. Yearning. Desire. Hunger.

Finally at the point where the red haze of lust had lifted, he purposely turned away from the door. Once he made it to the living room, the memory of how fucking sexy she looked standing in front of him just minutes ago hit him again.

His need for her was building more and more each moment they spent together. When first meeting Faith, he immediately noticed her beauty. Not classical, but seductive. Her face drew him to her and he couldn't look away—still can't. The lush curves of her body called out to him every time she accidentally brushed up against him, or when they touched or hugged. It was as if she pulled out some long buried desire to feel himself cradled between the thighs of a woman with soft flesh and meat on her bones, enough for him to grab onto as he pounded her body into oblivion.

God, he had it bad for this woman. It had been months of being near her, yet not being able to touch her the way he desired most. Fighting his desire had become a losing battle. Now, all he had to do was change things up. It was time to put her off her game.

Chapter Six

A week later, Cooper was sitting on the front porch watching the sun go down. Madison had been invited to a birthday party and had been gone for a few hours. Glancing at his watch, he noted the time and looked up the street to see if he could catch a glimpse of Madison and Faith. The party should be ending right about now and they were due back any moment.

Their neighborhood was teeming with activity and he watched kids ride bikes and skateboards up and down the street. Waving to those who waved at him, he smiled at the kids, and adults, who yelled out to him in greeting. Because of the season, it was still bright outside. In the distance, he could see a hint of the moon and stars that would soon light up the night sky.

"Hey there, Cooper," he was greeted by a couple he knew from neighborhood gatherings.

Standing up, he waved and walked over to greet them, "Hey, Tom. How are you, Susan? Enjoying the night air?

"Yeah," Tom answered, "the girls are over at the birthday party and we're on our way to get them now. Instead of driving, figured we would walk. That way, they can burn off any excess energy."

Laughing in solidarity, Cooper understood exactly what they were talking about, "Well, I'm fully expecting Madison to be bouncing off the walls when they get back. Faith should be bringing her back any minute now."

"Those two are really close. I know that must be good for Madison to have Faith in her life," Susan commented. "It would be a shame if Faith were to ever move away or want to have children of her own." Giving him a piercing look, she continued, "Well, we'd better go grab them before it gets to be too late. Tell Faith I said hi." Grabbing her husband's hand as they continued walking down the street, she turned back one more time, "I think we'll be having a get together in the next month or so. I'll make sure Tom brings over an invitation."

Nodding his head to Tom, who was rolling his eyes at his wife's perceived meddling, Cooper called out, "Okay, yeah, sounds good, Susan. Have a good night."

Although her words about Faith wanting children "of her own" were said as a seemingly general comment, they still bothered him. He and Faith hadn't talked about how things were changing between them. Not even once had they made the attempt to talk about what happened last week at his home. But she had to know how he felt about her, or at least that he was attracted to her. Seriously attracted to her.

He knew she had friends and went out occasionally after work. She even traveled for work on occasion. But not once, had she ever mentioned a man in her life until that date she went on a month ago. Rubbing his neck as he looked in the direction Tom and Susan had walked, his mind whirled with the possibilities. There was a gnawing feeling in his gut that if she did want to move on with someone—someone that was not him—he knew that wouldn't sit well with him at all.

Watching as the neighborhood kids played up and down the sidewalk and in the front yards of the houses that lined the streets, he thought he caught sight of Faith and Madison. His daughter had made the executive decision that Faith would be the one to take her to her friend's house for the birthday party, which had been okay with him. In actuality, he had been amused. Without either of them realizing it, his daughter had somehow adopted their neighbor and made her an unofficial part of their family.

"Daddy! Daddy! Look at what me and Ms. Faith got from the party!" Madison sprinted up the walkway in front of their home. Back on the porch and sitting in a deck chair, he caught her as she sprinted to him and leapt into his arms.

"Well, what do we have here?" Testing the weight of the bag of small gifts and toys that had been given out by her friend's parents, he turned wide eyes toward Madison. "This is heavy! How did you get this all the way home?"

"Faith helped me." Turning his head to look in her direction, he watched Faith trudge up the sidewalk. Giving her a slight smile as she waved her hand in his direction, he took pity on her. For about three seconds and then he started to smile. Her face bore an expression that all parents had in common on a day like this. Completely and utterly worn out. Smiling at the sight of her standing in front of him, he almost laughed out loud, but decided that would be a bad move. "Poor Faith, did Madison run you ragged?"

"Hardy-har-har! No. I'm full of energy. I could go another two hours." Getting to the top step, she slowly turned and sat down, "just let me nap for two days."

"Well, even if you're not tired, it's almost time for the little princess to get ready for bed." Pulling his daughter close, he peaked inside her bag to look at what she had brought home.

Madison's small hand reached up to his face and pulled him down, she then whispered close to his ear, "Daddy, I'm not tired."

"I know you're not, baby, but that doesn't mean you don't have to go to bed." Already knowing what the answer would be, Cooper asked the question anyway, "Did you and Faith have fun today?"

"We did. And guess what, Daddy? I have to tell you something," she whispered the last statement, which got his attention.

Sure that it was something about her friends or the party, he bent down to hear her secret, "What?"

"I love Faith, Daddy. I do! Can I tell her?" Her eyes were big and he could tell from her expression, that his daughter meant every single word. Damn. He probably should have realized this was happening. All the signs were there. It was inevitable that Madison would become connected so strongly to the woman that had, in effect, treated her like she was her own child.

Raising his eyes quickly, he glanced at Faith to see if she had heard her confession. When he saw that she was still lying on her back with her eyes closed, he figured that she had not picked up on their secret conversation. Oddly enough, he was equal parts relieved and disappointed.

Something in him was glad that Faith had not heard his daughter's confession because she may not feel the same. That type of rejection would be a difficult thing for a child to deal with, especially for a little girl who had lost her mother at such a young age. He had tried to do the best he could, but Madison clearly wanted—needed—something more than he could provide. What truly shocked him most was the feeling that he wanted to know if Faith really did love his daughter in return. And what if she did? Then what?

"How about you tell her another day?" Unable to get his voice low enough to prevent her overhearing, he felt Faith's gaze turn toward him and lifted his eyes to hers for just a second. Noticing her eyebrows raised in question, he shrugged and shook his head to stall any questions.

Looking back at his daughter, he could tell that she was not happy with his direction. Sometimes she could have a mind of her own and wasn't always receptive to being put in a box. That was definitely a personality trait she inherited from her mother. He would not take the blame for that one. Not this time. His next words were a bit louder, "Okay, princess, it's almost eight o'clock. It's time to get ready for bed."

"Awww, Dad. I don't want to." Jumping from his lap even as she spoke the words, she began making her way to the front door.

"I know, but little girls need their sleep" Voice light with laughter, he couldn't help looking over at Faith again. They had talked several times in the last few weeks about Madison's burgeoning need for independence. Catching Faith's gaze, they shared a moment of adult mirth at the logic and antics of a four-year old child, which they both succumbed to each and every time.

As Faith sat there laughing silently behind her hand, his smile became even wider as he gave thanks that she was there. Able to share this moment with him.

Looking around as if bored with the turn the conversation had taken, Madison quickly turned back to Faith. "Can you help me go to bed, Ms. Faith?"

Dark brown eyes turned to him in question. "Sure, honey, as long as your dad is okay with it."

"Are you okay, Daddy?" Not that she was actually waiting for his response. Already walking toward the door, she grabbed Faith's hand in her smaller one and began pulling her along.

"Yes, honey, that's fine. Faith, I'll be out here when you finish." Settling back in his seat, he noticed a few more kids outside playing and settled in to wait for Faith to return.

"Okay, see you in a bit," Faith called back at him. As they walked into the house, his ears picked up the echo of their voices. Quick footfalls on the stairs reverberated through the house and out the open window as they made their way to her bedroom. A feeling of peace overcame him. This is what he needed and it calmed him to know that Faith and Madison were both in his home.

No more than 30 minutes later, Faith exited the house and stood in front of the closed screen door for a few minutes. Looking back over her shoulder as if confused, her brow was furrowed in concern and she bit her bottom lip. Watching her silently for a few minutes, Cooper purposely ignored the invisible barrier holding him back from moving forward with his beautiful neighbor and took the time to really look at her.

Gazing at her as no longer just a neighbor and friend, but as a woman, his need for her began to surge. Without a doubt, he liked what he saw on the outside and wanted to explore more of the woman beneath the clothing. But now that he knew the woman behind the curves and sassy attitude, he felt something more than just a physical attraction.

Was he truly ready for this? Would the memory of his wife continue to press on him? Could he ask Faith to give herself over to a man who still had to ask himself that question? Deciding that he wouldn't be able to answer that question tonight, he put it on the backburner for another day. He instead focused on the woman standing in front of him.

"What's wrong, Faith?"

"Um, nothing really. I just…" Looking over her shoulder one more time, she slowly moved from her spot. Coming over next to him, she sat on the bench that was situated next to his chair.

Beginning to get concerned, he was about to get up and go into the house and check on Madison. Just as he was lifting up, the next words from Faith's mouth stopped him in his tracks.

"Madison is…," she paused and sighed deeply, "That little girl has stolen my heart. I love her so much. Do you know that?"

Instead of rushing into the house, he lifted out of his chair and went over to the bench, sitting next to Faith. "I know you do. I see it every time you're with her." Knowing his daughter had not heeded his direction to wait to share her confession, he continued, "But what made you say it tonight? To me?"

Cooper didn't think she realized it at the time, but when she began to answer the question, she grabbed his hand in hers. "Upstairs, as she was getting into bed, she said she loved me." The joy on her face was his undoing. How could a woman who had not birthed a child, feel so much joy and happiness at the knowledge of that child's love for them?

"Did this upset you?" Based on her response, he would hazard a guess to say no, but he wanted to hear her say it.

"Oh, no! Absolutely not. I know she lost her mother and for a little girl, that can be traumatic."

Cooper interrupted, "Has she ever talked about her mother? Asked questions?"

She shook her head no, still holding onto his hand as she continued, "Not really. I mean, she sometimes looks at mothers and daughters with a little more curiosity. Occasionally, she'll make comments about things her and her mommy would do if she were alive." Pausing for a moment, she looked out over the yard, "The time I've spent with her has been because I wanted to do it. Just because she is such a caring and open child. It was just…I don't know. Hearing the words made me realize that she has come to mean so much to me."

He knew that Madison's curiosity and observations about her mother, or lack thereof, was natural. The counselors and therapists he had spoken with had told him so. "Well, from what I've been told, when she does bring up Heather, it's important to let her questions and comments flow naturally. I've tried to be careful not to force any conversation about her mother, but also not shy away from it when she wants to talk."

Looking at the woman sitting next to him in a new light, he began to understand what was starting to happen, "It seems that you've become someone she feels that she can trust. Someone she knows she can be herself with and not hide."

"She's an amazing little girl. I will never overstep, Cooper, but I will be here for Madison. For however long she needs me, I will always be a part of her life," she answered him.

"I know you will and I appreciate that." Placing his other hand over their already joined hands, he gave a little squeeze. She jumped slightly, as if just noticing that she already had his hand in hers. Moving slightly as if to release herself from his grasp and pull away, he stopped her movement by holding on a little tighter.

Leaning back, he waved at some of the passersby heading back to their respective homes for the evening. This was good. It felt right. It had been a good night for everyone. He felt as if things were moving in the right direction.

His little girl was happy. He was damn close to being happy. And his beautiful, lovely neighbor was sitting here, next to him. Their hands joined and the two of them simply relaxing. Quiet surrounded them as they sat nestled on his front porch as the night closed in around them. This was what he missed. This is what he needed.

"This is nice, Cooper." Faith's soft voice reached him as he considered the possibilities of where this could go.

"Yes, it is. I haven't enjoyed a night like this in a long time." Removing his hand from hers, he adjusted slightly. Wrapping his arms around her shoulders, he pulled her soft body into his, bringing her closer to him.

"I'm too heavy to be leaning on you, Cooper." She tried to lift some of her weight off of him.

"No, you're not. Stop that nonsense talk, woman. Just relax and lean on me. I'm more than strong enough to hold you and you know it. If you want me to prove it, just say the word, sweetheart," he laughed in response.

Cooper knew she was talking about her weight and he wasn't going to allow her to get away with that. On one or two occasions, he had heard her refer to her weight. Once or twice she had commented that she felt she was too big to do something, or wear some piece of clothing. After seeing her almost every day since they had moved in, he had enjoyed looking at every curve of her body and disagreed wholeheartedly. Faith was an exceedingly sexy woman and any man would be lucky to have her. Although if he had his way, there would be no other man vying for her attention. No one except for him, that is.

∞ ∞ ∞ ∞ ∞

Later that week, Cooper was sitting next to Faith as the three of them relaxed at her house. A trip to the local park had been the original plan, but the weather had not cooperated. It turned out to be a rainy, dreary day, so they all decided it was best to order pizza and watch a movie. Of course, as long as Madison was around Faith, he knew that she would be happy with whatever they decided to do.

Still reeling from the events of the last two weeks, Cooper was analyzing what was happening to him. His feelings for Faith had been growing rapidly for some time now. Thinking of her as more than just a friend had begun shortly after he met her. Hearing her laugh, made him smile. Watching her walk toward him made him hard. Whatever it was, he knew it was real for him. It wasn't that he was lonely and it wasn't some rebound or passing phase. Not for him. There had been some women in the past two years that he had seen casually, but only recently had he actually considered the idea of dating just one woman.

He had begun dating a few months ago at the behest of some of his Army buddies who were still in the area. A few of his first dates had turned into a second date. Some resulted in a night cap, which usually turned into an overnight stay. Inevitably, that would end with him sliding out of the woman's bedroom, and any need to see them again in the future leaving right along with him.

While he wouldn't say he was proud of his behavior, he was honest. They knew what he offered and had no expectations of anything beyond that. At no time had he ever been careless and not worn protection, nor had he given them false promises. Just a mutual agreement that they would enjoy their time together. Luckily, none of them had turned stalkerish or had a hard time getting the message. Well, except for Dana. God, that was painful and he never wanted to go through that again.

Putting the memory aside, he looked over and saw that Madison had gotten up from the floor and was now sprawled on Faith's chaise lounge. For such a small child, she sure had a strong sense of self-confidence. She was giggling at the movie playing on the television and Faith was watching her with a smile on her face.

He wondered what she thought of when she looked at them, the carefree and precocious daughter and the sometimes moody father who seemed locked in the past, holding on to the memory of a wife, of a life, that no longer existed.

If truth be told, he held more than just a passing affection for his lovely neighbor. Although he actively tried to temper how he showed this to Faith, or heaven forbid, his daughter. One whiff of something more between he and Faith and he was positive his daughter would shout it from the rooftop.

Long out of his teenage years, he knew it wouldn't look good if he started behaving as if he were in high school with a crush on the prettiest girl in class. Then again, he was probably thinking about this much more than he needed to.

Cooper could admit, at least to himself, that these last few months had been really good. Not just for him, but for Madison. Sitting here with Faith always seemed comfortable. There was no pressure. No need to try and be something he wasn't. With her, he could just be himself. That hadn't happened for a long time and he missed this feeling. Although he would deny it until the cows came home, this felt right to him. Even if they had never been intimate, the feeling that this is where he belonged was clamoring away in his head.

As he looked over at her sitting just a few feet away from him, he took a minute to admire her. Wearing shorts since it was a warm day, most of her legs were visible to his gaze. Silently looking at her womanly form, he could admire the curve of her thigh and the smoothness of her shoulder as she typed on her laptop.

He did wonder why he hadn't made a move on her before the other night. Tried to at least kiss those full lips of hers? Remembering the other night when they had returned from the kite festival in DC, and the moans of pleasure she made as he massaged her feet, he couldn't help but think he had missed what was right in front of him this entire time. Maybe it was her closeness to Madison that had stopped him before.

If he did try to gauge her interest in him sexually, or if they slept together and things didn't work out, how would that impact Madison? No, he couldn't risk it right now. She was a fixture in his daughter's life and his baser nature, no matter how much it called out to him, was not going to ruin it.

Faith gave both him and Madison something...someone...that they looked forward to seeing every day. Early on, just after they had moved in, Faith had taken to calling Madison by her special name, princess, which Madison had noticed right away. Since then, the two of them had built their own relationship together, exclusive of Cooper. The connection between those two was so strong, and after spending so much time at each other's house, he could almost feel their bond getting stronger.

There had even been a pampering weekend, or ten, when Faith and Madison had gone to the local spa for what she called mani/pedi treatments, her words—not his. His ears had almost bled from listening to his daughter talk about the fun they had, how the staff treated her like a princess, and how amazing Ms. Faith was. Slowly, but surely, there were other slight changes that now looking back, he had taken for granted.

When at her house on any given night, he would see his favorite beer sitting in her fridge. Just waiting for him. She never drank the stuff, so he knew it wasn't for her. Two extra plates always seemed to be ready and filled to the brim each night they came over, as if she knew they would be there. Faith had even picked up his moods. Ever so smoothly, they had built a friendship and connection that was comfortable, and they simply seemed to fit.

However, just last night, the closeness the three of them shared had caused a mini-meltdown for Madison. As he was putting his little girl down for the night, he mentioned their trip to Rehoboth Beach with his mother and some other family members. It had been a family tradition for everyone to meet in Delaware to reunite and have some fun before winter hit. Realizing now that he should have considered the ramifications of thinking like a man, it had failed to dawn on him that Faith wouldn't be there. After all, he had forgotten to even mention it to her, so why would she? Once he realized this, it seemed Madison wasn't far behind.

When Madison finally understood Faith was not going to be coming with them, she was not happy. Not one little bit. Sitting here looking over at the woman who had created such high loyalty in his little girl, he knew he had to talk with her about it tonight. Cringing a little as he thought back on last night's conversation with Madison, he almost wished Faith would come with them. His own procrastination had caused this and he knew it. The conversation with his daughter replayed in his mind.

"Why can't Ms. Faith come with us to Grandma's house?" Mouth turned down and eyes filling with tears, his little girl was not very pleased with him at the moment.

"Because Faith has her own family and friends. I'm sure they want her to spend the holiday with them," he responded as calmly as he could. Getting Madison to understand that Faith didn't belong to only them was becoming harder each day.

Then again, he had his own issues with that lately. Not thinking straight, he had made his own assumptions and hadn't even considered that he needed to ask Faith. Looking back, he knew he had fucked this up royally.

Lately though, it seemed that Faith was just always there. Which is what he enjoyed most. When he wanted to see her, he did. When coming home from work at night, if he called and she wasn't home, he texted. As soon as she responded, he made sure to ask when she would be home. While he always used the excuse that Madison was the one who wanted to see her before going to bed, he also knew that it was something he needed as well.

Seeing her, even just to spend five minutes talking with her each day, had become something he needed to do each night before he could relax and fall asleep. Recalling his daughter's voice as she continued her pleas for Faith to join them for the long weekend, he had continued tucking her in under the covers.

"But she has to come with us. You have to ask her," clearly not giving up her request, Madison continued to press the issue.

Cooper had to understand that with Madison being so young, she didn't understand how complicated adult lives could be. So, he agreed, sort of, "Okay, I will ask her tomorrow. But if she says no, then that's the final answer. Understand?" He would swear his little girl was smarter than her four years as she looked at him with suspicion.

"You promise to ask her," she inquired.

"Promise. Now go to sleep," he kissed her on the forehead and exited the room. Laughing to himself as he turned out the hallway lights and entered his own bedroom, he wondered if Faith really had any plans for the weekend. Would it be such a big deal if she came with them? They were only friends, right?

Chapter Seven

Now here he was the next evening, sitting near Faith as they relaxed after dinner. Still not having broached the subject, he was tempted to just leave it alone and not ask. He wasn't usually this damn nervous, but lately, something had changed. His Special Forces buddies, and even the people he worked with now, would never believe this. They always described him as hard, unforgiving, candid, brutal, and even aggressive. They would laugh in his face if they knew he was fretting about a woman's response to such an inane thing. But with this woman, none of that mattered. Over the years, he had become a cold, heartless killing machine. But with Faith, he seemed to lose all of that.

His cool points balance took a deduction each day that he was in her presence. Five points every time he called her before he went to bed. Another ten points whenever he became tongue-tied around her when she had on her black yoga pants and a t-shirt. Heaven forbid his friends ever find out that he spent an entire afternoon looking through paints and fabric patterns when she wanted to redecorate her upstairs guest room. It was downright odd! And if he wasn't careful, he would continue to get deeper, which was something he couldn't do.

Resolved to get this over and done with, Cooper excused himself.

"I'll be back. I'm headed to the kitchen. Do you want a drink, Madison?"

"No, Daddy," she responded and then giggled at a scene in the movie.

Tapping Faith's arm, he nodded at her to follow him and started walking toward the other room. Once in the kitchen, he leaned up against the counter and watched as Faith came into the room a few seconds after he did.

His eyes were drawn to her shapely legs and her toes painted in a vibrant pink, the result of a recent spa day for her and Madison. Eyes going to her face, he noticed that her smooth brown skin seemed to glow with vitality. Her lips were tilted in a mischievous smile and her walk was...damn. Hips swaying from side-to-side, he could feel his body begin to react to her and had to adjust his stance. Three words entered his head and he knew that it was the unfiltered truth.

So fucking beautiful.

Stopping just inches in front of him, Faith hopped up to sit on the three-legged stool in front of the breakfast nook. Sitting there with a questioning look on her face, she began to fidget as she waited for him to speak.

Smiling, Cooper realized how common this scene had become. Maybe it wouldn't be such a big deal if she came with him. And after his recent train of thoughts about her, he was quickly coming to the conclusion that he wanted Faith to come with them for their family weekend. By all accounts, she was already part of their family. What would make the weekend in Rehoboth Beach any different?

Although he had told Madison that Faith probably had other plans, he wasn't so sure that was true. Hell, if he were actually honest with himself, he didn't want it to be true. It would be nice to have her with them, on his own territory for four full days. She could spend time getting to know his family and maybe, just maybe, he could figure out why his thoughts about the one person who had become his closest friend, had become focused on getting her out of her clothes and into his bed.

Before he could dissect why having Faith spend time getting to know his family made him smile, she interrupted his thoughts.

"What's up, buttercup? You wanted me to come in here, right?" she asked jokingly. Chuckling at her own corny and warped sense of humor, she suddenly gave him a wide smile and began laughing.

Interrupting her one-person comedy show, he shared the reason for their impromptu meeting. "So, Madison wants you to come with us to her Grandmother's house for Labor Day."

What? He wasn't fool enough to say that he wanted her there as well.

At her stunned response, he continued, "So, what do you think? Want to come spend the Labor Day weekend with us?" He fully expected her to jump at the chance to spend time with them and found that he was excited at the prospect. They could explore this thing that was building up between them.

Turns out, he was in for a surprise.

After a few moments of silence, her face turned down for a brief moment, as if she had become saddened by the question. Faith then smiled, just a tiny lift of the corners of her mouth, and then turned him down flat, "Actually, I can't. I'm sorry, Cooper."

"Oh, great…wait! What?" Not sure that he heard her right, he had to stop and think for a few seconds to process her words. “What do you mean you can’t? Why not?”

The words came out a bit harsher than he expected them to, but that couldn’t be helped. Noticing her response, he could tell she had not been expecting that response. Taking a half-step back, he waited for her to tell him why she couldn’t go with them. Where the hell else would she be?

Sitting up a bit straighter on the stool, her eyes were cold as she responded, “Well, I wasn’t expecting to see you guys that weekend, so I made plans. I’m going down to Miami to see an old college friend.” Hearing the flat tone of her voice, he could tell that she was not happy with how he responded.

“You never mentioned that before,” he responded.

“Well, you never asked,” she replied in turn.

“Dammit, Faith, I didn’t know that I needed to!” He hadn’t meant to yell, but he had never expected her to tell him no. She had never denied him anything—ever. This shit was throwing him off, big time. Fuck! Never expecting her answer to be no, he wasn’t quite sure how to respond to this new development.

Then again, why was this such a shock to his system? Wasn’t he already expecting her to have plans? There was no rule that said she needed to spend all of her time with him and Madison. But still, he didn’t like the feeling he was having about this. It felt a lot like jealousy.

“Okay, what is this all about? When did you start expecting me to clear my schedule with you?” Faith was leaning back, her elbows on the counter and her feet crossed. The smile that he had come to expect and enjoy so much was nowhere to be seen.

Trying to recover and avoid coming off as an even bigger ass, he tried to sound neutral as he responded, "Fine. You don't. It was just...never mind. Just forget it." Based on the look that was reflected on her face, he hadn't done a very good job of glossing over how he felt. Trying another tactic, "Well, I just wanted to mention it to you as an option. For Madison."

"Cooper, I can change my plans if you want me to," she tried to interject, but to him, it was too late.

"No, it's fine. We can always do something on our own, before Madison and I go up there," he said.

It suddenly hit him that the upcoming holiday weekend would be the longest they had been away from each other since they had met. At least by choice. Each of them had traveled for work in the past few months, but that had always been something they couldn't avoid. Work was work. Out of town business travel was one thing. Choosing to go to different vacation spots on a major holiday by choice? Well, that felt entirely different. What the hell had happened to him and why didn't he see this coming?

"Okay. If you're sure," she said hesitantly.

He wasn't sure at all, but neither did he have a choice it seemed. "I'm sure you'll have a great time." Not willing to play the role of forgiving friend, he simply didn't respond to the unanswered questions he was sure she had.

Smirking to himself, he thought, 'I hope it rains during her entire Miami visit.' Picturing the thought of her trip ending up a complete and total washout, literally, had him feeling quite a bit better. She would look back and wish that she had chosen to come with him and Madison. Shaking away the internal thought, he knew that it was completely selfish of him to think that way. He just wanted her there with them and not over a thousand miles away.

"What are you smiling about, Cooper?" She asked slowly.

Eyeing her as she sat her on the stool, he couldn't stop the next question, "Will you miss us?" Nope, not even if he had tried.

Recognizing that things were changing for him, for them, he made the decision to at least test things out. See how Faith would respond if he pushed things a little further than normal.

Dark brown eyes stared at him for a few seconds. If he had to wait for an hour to hear her response, that's what he would do. Awareness hit him like a twenty pound brick. Would she miss them—him—as much as he would miss her?

"Of course, I will," her response came out low, as if she were hesitant to speak the words.

Shifting slightly, he turned to her just as she came off the stool and stood in front of him. In her bare feet, she stood six inches shorter than him and he liked her this way. Brown eyes met light blue and he felt, more than saw, her breathing become jagged and shallow as they stood in front of one other.

"I'll miss you, too. Surely you must know that," the honesty of his words didn't escape his notice as he spoke what he truly felt.

At her sudden intake of breath and the widening of her eyes, he knew the exact moment Faith understood as well.

There was no more hiding from what was happening between them. His nice, structured world had evolved and become something completely different, and Faith had a starring role. Both he and Faith were guilty of ignoring the signs that were flashing bright red in front of their eyes. There was no turning back and Cooper was ready.

With the truth staring him in the face, he knew, without a doubt, that he wanted this woman with every fiber of his being. He wasn't sure how long he could hold back and not simply seduce her into his bed. Sex was one thing and he had never been without someone that could help relieve stress. After his wife's death, once he returned to the land of the living, there had been plenty of women lined up to offer him whatever he needed, desired, or was simply curious enough to try.

But none of them were her. None of them affected him the way Faith did. And he didn't think she even tried. It was just her. This was a different feeling for him. While he was positive that he would do everything in his power to please her, to make her body weep with anticipation for him, it would be a huge step. Before he made this step with her, Cooper needed to first let go of the past and grab ahold of his future with both hands.

Actually, there was a larger question lingering in the air. Was Faith ready for him? He didn't think she had any clue about the lion that was ready to be unleashed on her. But she would learn soon enough. Some would assume that they had already crossed the line and become intimate with each other. If truth be known, he and Faith had never even shared a kiss. But if he had anything to say about it, that would change soon enough.

The moment seemed to pass by in slow motion. Having her this close, the space between them seemed to sizzle with electricity. Maybe this had been building for a while. The two of them lived a life that centered on each other. But deep inside, could he truly say that he was ready to move on with his life and leave the past behind? Was it possible to allow himself to fully open up and let Faith take her place by his side?

He was bothered by the thought that there was still too much of his past with Heather holding on to him. It wouldn't be fair to Faith to come at her now. Not while he was still in the process letting go.

But now that he took time to think about it, the hurt and pain that usually came when he thought about putting his past behind him, never materialized. Would Heather really expect him to never fall in love again? To never feel desire for another woman? Or feel the soft curves of her body as he sank inside of her? He couldn't see her denying him the chance to be happy again.

Faith was all he ever thought about, aside from his daughter. She was the first person he thought of in the morning. She was the last person he thought of before he went to bed. He should have seen what was happening a long time ago.

Picturing Faith beneath him, her legs spread wide as he stroked in and out of her body made sweat bead on his upper lip. Unbidden, the idea of bringing them both to the heights of pleasure entered his mind. It was enough to make his body heat from the inside-out.

And even though her body language was sending him a message that he so desperately wanted to respond to, he didn't. No matter how much he may have wanted to lean down and brush his lips against hers, he wouldn't. Not yet. This was Faith and she deserved all of him, not some sliver of a man that held on to the ghosts of his past.

The few seconds they stood there staring at each other seemed like hours. Would one little kiss hurt? Just a little nibble to see if her lips tasted as good as they looked. Unashamed and unapologetic, his gaze soaked in the sight of the woman before him and he refused to turn away. There would be no more denying what he wanted.

The television played in the background. Loud sounds of cartoon characters traveled from the living room where his daughter continued to sit as she played with her toys. When it was all said and done, that was the thought that made him pull back. Taking a step away from Faith, the tether holding them was broken.

Things seemed to calm and the spell they had been under had evaporated into the space between them. They each looked at one another as if meeting for the first time.

Faith was the first one to speak, "We had better go back in the other room. She'll come looking for us soon."

For a moment, words failed him. How could he feel so strongly for her in what some would think was such a short time? It had taken him more than a year to feel this way about Heather and that unnerved him. "Yeah, I guess we should."

Shaking his head in slight disbelief, he thought, she's not really even my type, but no one else does it for me like her. Faith was the only woman that he had allowed to get close to him since his wife died. So whether or not he thought she was his type or not, was a moot point. Clearly his dick and his heart wanted her with a fierceness that would not be denied.

"Are you sure you can't make it to Rehoboth Beach with us?" As she turned to walk out of the kitchen, he couldn't resist asking one more time. Maybe this time would be different. Everything in him wanted to yell out, 'Dammit, woman, just say yes', but he was smart enough to know that would be a bad move.

Pausing before she answered, he was almost hopeful that she had seen the error of her ways and would be coming with them after all. Decide that the best place for her was to be with him, instead of hundreds of miles away in a city known for its hedonism. After all, they needed to explore what had just happened, what had been happening, between them. It would not be easy for him to have her away from them, several states away, doing God knows what. And just who the hell was this old college friend she was meeting up with?

"Faith, who—", he was about to ask who she was going to meet in Miami when she spoke at the same time.

Faith's voice interrupted his thoughts, "No, I think it would be best for me to head down to Miami. I'm sure you two will have a great time without me."

And with that, she walked out of the room, leaving him standing there by himself. Alone. Jealous. Frustrated. And very, very confused about the depth of the feelings he had for his sexy neighbor.

There had to be a way to stop her from going down to Miami. She may not realize it yet, but he was a man on a mission. And that mission had a name.

Faith.

Chapter Eight

Faith's life had changed so much in the last few months. Some good. Some bad. Some things...well, she was still deciding how to react to them. She was no longer on her own and she loved every minute of her new way of life. It was always Cooper, Faith, and Madison, in that order. Even when attending their neighborhood events, it was always the three of them. It was just expected.

If Madison drew a picture for Cooper, she drew one for Faith. If Faith was at the house when Madison went to bed at night, she had to read her story before she fell asleep. When Faith had to work late or travel out-of-state on business, Madison called her every night. Mainly to tell her about her day before she went to bed, but Faith loved every minute of their conversations. She had even taken to including Faith in the family drawings that included her, Cooper and her Angel Mommy in Heaven, as Madison referred to her birth mother.

For all intents and purposes, Faith was already a part of their family in every way that counted the most. Except that she wasn't, nor did she expect to ever be, a loving partner to Cooper. At least not until a few weeks ago when things had seemed to change between them.

Walking back into the living room, she glanced behind her to see where Cooper was. She gasped when she saw the look in his eyes. No, that was definitely not the look of a platonic friend. His eyes were full of meaning and they were focused slowly on her retreating form.

"Where have you been, Faith? You and daddy took forever," she almost jumped out of her skin as Madison started speaking. Leave it up to the little imp to call them both out.

"We were in the kitchen. Um, we were trying to decide what we should do before you and your dad go to the beach," she responded, trying to get the little girl's mind off of what had taken them so long.

"But, aren't you coming too?" Her bottom lip began to poke out and quiver. "I told daddy I wanted you there with us. Why can't you come?"

"Oh, honey, come up here." Pulling the little girl up from the chaise lounge, she turned and sat down herself. Lifting Madison onto her lap, she gave her a hug. "I would if I could, but I'm going somewhere else."

"But why? You don't like the beach?" The sadness in Madison's voice broke her heart.

"I love the beach. We'll all go together another time. How about that?" Faith really wanted to get her off of this topic.

"Do you not want to be around us anymore?" Oh no, where did that question come from? Faith wasn't sure how she was going to win this battle.

Squeezing her arms around the little girl even tighter, she gave her a kiss on the forehead, "Oh, Princess, of course I do. I love spending time with you. You're my partner-in-crime and that's never going to change."

"But then who are you going with?" She was like a detective.

"Well, a friend of mine that I haven't seen in a long, long time lives down there. He wants me to come visit him since we haven't seen each other for a while," she responded with the truth. "But I will be back here before you know it and we can have a picnic." Hoping that last statement would make it all better, she waited patiently for Madison to respond.

"Promise?"

Faith sighed in relief, "I promise, sweetheart."

Feeling a tingling sensation on the back of her neck, she looked up and saw Cooper standing in the entrance to the room. Lips turned up in a scowl, all she could think was that he looked pissed. He must have heard the entire conversation, but what reason would he have to be upset? Arthur truly was just a friend. Someone she had known back in college. They had never been "like that" with each other and never would.

Considering she was a single woman and Cooper had no claim on her, he could be as upset as he wanted to. She wasn't changing her plans because he felt threatened that she had a life outside of him. If he wanted more from her, then he needed to step up to plate.

And aside from that little interlude in the kitchen just now…and the other week after the trip to Washington, DC, she admitted begrudgingly, he hadn't done anything to show her that he truly wanted more. That their flirtation was more than just two friends who were in close proximity to each other. Sometimes, she wondered how she had gotten into this mess. Falling in love with a man who was still in love with his deceased wife had not been her best move.

Deciding to ignore Cooper, she turned back to Madison. That man could get glad in the same underwear he got mad in. She was not doing this with him tonight. Just because she had always been there for him in the past, didn't mean she would stay that way. She had a life too and she would be damned if he would try to prevent that.

Picking up the remote control from where it sat on the coffee table, she turned up the television. Trying valiantly to ignore the man who had caused her numerous sleepless nights, she purposely looked away from him. It took all her willpower not to turn around and ask him why he was just standing there staring a hole in the back of her head.

After a few more seconds, he gave up and stomped back into the kitchen. His heavy footsteps hinting at his level of frustration. Good! Now he could feel a little of what she had been going through.

When she and Cooper had first met, it had been lust at first sight. At least for her it was. Not usually prone to jumping to conclusions, she found herself doodling his name while sitting in meetings. Or she found that she was prone to waiting for that first glimpse of him each day. For a grounded woman in her early thirties, she had become giddy at the thought of her and Cooper as a couple. A naked, sweaty, loving all night long until the sun came up type of couple. It was completely out of character for her, but that hadn't made the thoughts go away.

But no matter what happened and no matter how many times she may have wished he'd look at her as more than just a friend, it just hadn't come to be. They had lived next to each other for all these months and other than their first embarrassing meeting, she had been very careful to not make any risky moves. That didn't mean she hadn't given him a hug that lasted a second too long. Or ran her hands through his hair as they were hanging out at the park, or even while sitting on the front porch watching Madison play with her friends.

Cooper had never given any real inkling of being attracted to her, other than to remark on her appearance in a general sense, as any gentleman would. There were those moments when it had been only the two of them, when things seemed just right. Perfectly situated for something to change, for the moment to flip. Whether they were sitting on the porch swing out front or at the dining room table after a meal. She could almost feel something bubbling to the surface, waiting to break free.

Just as she would begin to peel back the layers and gather enough bravado to address the elephant in the room, something would always happen. Some interruption would occur to end the moment and the opportunity would slip through her hands. Or, even worse, seconds...minutes would simply pass by without a word being said between the two of them. Usually because she was too chicken-shit to risk putting her foot in her mouth.

He had even gone on a few dates and asked her to watch Madison. Those had not been fun nights for her. Waiting. Wondering. Praying that her overly dramatic mind was completely and utterly wrong.

They were very close friends and she loved that about their relationship. That was one part of her world that she never wanted to change. They spent almost all their free time together. Finishing each other's sentences had become a running joke. Cooper never failed to anticipate her needs, even when she was in a total funk. It was new and different, and somewhat refreshing, to only be friends without the sex mixed in. Some marriages had lasted for less time than their friendship and she would be smart to not mess that up.

Then again, her growing desire for Cooper, that elusive need to have something more with him, almost broke her heart. How she longed to tell him that her feelings for him went deeper than he knew. If only she were brave enough to just blurt out the words and let him know that she wanted morc. Maybe it was just wishful thinking on her part.

When he asked her to go the beach with them for a family trip, she was so tempted to say yes. Telling him no had been one of the hardest things she'd had to do. Everything in her screamed out that this was the moment. That she should jump at this chance. But the offer from Arthur had been real. Only thing was, she hadn't actually told him yes. At least not yet.

Maybe it was time to shake things up a bit. Maybe Cooper needed to understand what he had right in front of him before it was too late.

∞ ∞ ∞ ∞ ∞

Faith had managed to avoid Cooper for almost a week. Every time he would call, she would try to avoid picking up. Not one to be deterred, he would then text her. Asking her question like where she was and when would she be home.

It was hard to keep making up excuses about work. Yes, she was busy, but at this point, they both knew that she was trying to avoid him.

And damn right she was trying to avoid him! That look in his eyes the other week had her panties soaking. It took everything in her not to strip naked and beg him to take her right then and there. The only thing stopping her was that she didn't believe the desire was real. They had been spending too much time in each other's company. Coupled with their closeness, it probably seemed like they "should" be having sex.

He had even asked her about the date she went on a few weeks ago. Madison had a playdate with a friend and the parent's would be bringing her home around seven. Cooper had come to her house and asked her to sit outside with him. At first she thought it was odd, but his reasons became clear soon enough.

"Who was the guy you went out with the other night," he opened.

Thrown off by the question, she didn't immediately know what, or who, he was referring to. "I didn't go on a date the other night."

Glancing at her sideways, he asked his question again, "Fine. A month ago. You remember Faith. It was the night you came home at almost midnight. The night I couldn't reach you. Who was he?"

Firing question after question at her about who he was, what he did for a living, where did they go, did she like him, and was she going to see him again? It had been daunting and he was determined to get the answers to his questions. She could see how he was such a good leader in his military Special Forces unit. The man was an unstoppable force when focused on something.

Hackles rising at the tone of his voice and the questions he asked, she fired back, "Why do you care? It's none of your business who I choose to date."

Taking a deep breath, she interrupted him just as he was going to ask another question, "Do I ask you about the women you date? Have I ever stuck my nose in your business, even when you ask me to watch Madison?" In her anger, her voice had risen a few levels and she was practically yelling at him. "Well, have I?"

He looked out over her front yard as she glared at his profile. Bending over at the waist, he placed his elbows on his knees, his voice was tight with what she could only assume was anger, "I didn't like it. And I can't get it out of my head."

Glancing at her, his face was no longer pinched in anger, but now his eyes looked tortured.

"Can't get what out of your head, Cooper?" Unsure if she wanted to know the answer, she asked the question anyway.

"The thought of another man holding you in his arms, kissing you," he replied. Lips pursed tightly, he reluctantly answered her question.

Shocked into silence, her mouth unable to form words, as he continued baring his soul to her as they sat on her front porch. The warm sun was setting and it provided the illusion of a normal night. This was becoming anything but that.

"I know I have no right to say these things to you. It doesn't make any sense for me to feel this way. I know that, but it doesn't change anything." Sitting back up, he took a deep breath. Rubbing his hands together rapidly, he then placed one on his thigh and the other rubbed the back of his neck. It was a nervous habit she had picked up on a few weeks ago.

"Cooper, I can't sit here and wait for you to decide what you want. I won't." Tears were forming in her eyes, but she refused to let them fall. How dare he give her the words she wanted to hear, but refuse to acknowledge the reasons? "And if I recall, just the other night, you asked me to watch Madison this weekend while you went on a date. Again!"

She stood up from the bench, her body shaking as she tried to calm down. "How dare you! You come to my house, telling me that you don't want me to date anyone. That you can't stand the thought of another man touching me. Yet, days later, you will be doing that very thing to another woman."

"Listen to me, Faith. It didn't come out right. I know I can't dictate what you do with your life," he said while reaching up one hand to her.

"No, you listen to me. Until you get your shit together and make a choice, we're just friends. I won't be anyone's second choice, Cooper. Either you want to stay married to the memory of your late wife, or you want the real thing. A living, breathing woman." Taking a breath, she calmed her voice as she looked at him staring at her with eyes widened in shock. "Cooper, I'm not saying what your choice has to be. But you do have to make a choice. Live in the past or build a new future. It's your choice. But if I'm not here waiting for you when you finally decide, then so be it."

His blue eyes darkened and his brow furrowed in anger. "Faith, you can't ask me to make that choice. I need time to do what's right."

"No, you don't Cooper. You know what's right. You know what you want. All you have to do is take a leap of faith. Until then, go home. I'll see you on

Saturday when you drop off Madison," she said sadly. Unable to hide how she was feeling, the hurt and pain came through loud and clear.

"I'll cancel. It was a setup by an Army buddy. It means nothing," he responded.

"No, you should go. This is not an ultimatum. This a friend giving you some much needed advice. You can't continue to live in the past, Cooper, or else you miss the future that's standing right in front of you." Walking past him was one of the hardest things she'd ever have to do. Closing the door behind her, she looked out the curtains every once in a while and still he sat. For more than thirty minutes he stayed there, sitting silently as the sun began to dip behind the horizon.

A few minutes before Madison was due home, he stood and left. Not once looking back.

Chapter Nine

Saturday night had finally come and Faith was on edge. After their conversation on the front porch, she and Cooper had only seen each other once. She had made lasagna for dinner on Thursday night and it had been way too much food for her, but instead of walking over some dinner for them to eat, she had just put it away in the fridge for leftovers. Plus, she hated the tension that had built up between the two of them.

If he were so upset about her going on a date with another man, why couldn't he understand how she felt? Offering to cancel his date was not the same thing as never going in the first place. Then again, she couldn't throw stones. Her date with John was still a barrier between them. Still not understanding why he was so intent to understand her reasons for going on a date, she was tempted to think he had been jealous. It had been a nice evening, but she and John hadn't even kissed good night. She had been too worried about how it would look to Cooper when he found out. And she had been right.

Looking at the clock and noting the time, she worried her bottom lip with her top teeth. There was no way in hell she was going to get through this night intact. Her tough exterior was just that, a shell. In reality, she was a sap for romance and happily-ever-after. Once she had fallen for Cooper, there had been no one else.

Then why did you tell him you were going to Miami? Isn't that the same thing? Is that the right thing? Visiting another man, even if it's not romantic?

Questions related to her own behavior ran through her mind and she could no longer deny the truth. She had been wrong. There was no way in hell she would be going to Miami and she knew it. A phone call to Arthur would be in order to let him know she would have to pass on his generous offer. She just hoped his fiancé would understand why she had to bail on them at such short notice.

Although she wasn't a glutton for punishment, she couldn't get Denise's hateful words from their botched lunch almost four months ago out of her mind. Although a very sexual woman, she wasn't foolish enough to think men did not see her as a sexual object. This wasn't her first time at the rodeo and neither was she an innocent. It had taken her years to get to where she was, to a place where she was confident in the woman she portrayed to the world.

In one day, no—one hour—she had allowed a back-stabbing friend to set her back by years. She had never questioned her value before and she sure as shit wasn't going to start now. But a fear of the future now held her in his grip. Now that she had found someone that not only made her feel whole—not only as a woman, but as a person—she had proof that it had to have been a moment of weakness. None of it had been real, and that's what hurt the most.

How did she know it wasn't real? Because Cooper had a date. Tonight. With a woman who wasn't her. All that talk about cancelling and how it meant nothing, was just that. Talk.

"Oh, Cooper, don't you see? I want something more with you," she murmured under her breath. Standing in front of the stove, she was stirring some creamy macaroni and cheese. An entire night of bad food, nail polish, and games were in order for her and Madison's upcoming girl's night.

Looking at the clock again and seeing that only five minutes had passed, she sighed. Noting that it was almost seven o'clock, she turned the heat down and went to put on the cartoon channel for Madison. That would entertain her for at least a few minutes when she arrived. The knock on the door sounded loudly in the room just as the show came back from a commercial.

Peeking out the side window to confirm it was Cooper, she swung the door open, a big, fake smile on her face. And she immediately regretted the decision to wear her comfortable in-house relaxation clothes. Cooper looked amazing. Wearing a dark grey suit with a light pink shirt that complimented his skin tone, he looked sexy as sin. No man had the right to look so good. He wasn't wearing a tie and the first two buttons of his shirt were undone, allowing her to glimpse, just a peak of his bare skin.

Had he ever looked this good for her? No, her mind yelled. No, he had not.

"Hi, Faith! I'm here!" Although quite unnecessary, Madison announced her presence. Loudly.

Stepping back to let them into the house, she bent down to give the little ball of energy a kiss on the cheek. "Hey, princess, I have your favorite show playing on the television."

"Okay. Bye, Daddy. I'm with Faith now. You can leave." Dismissing both adults just that easily, she ran into the living room and plopped down on the floor. Chin resting on her hands, she began singing one of the opening songs.

Faith couldn't help but smile. No matter how bad she was feeling, Madison could always cheer her up. Her father, on the other hand, was a different story.

"Thanks, Faith, I appreciate you watching her tonight," his voice broke into her thoughts.

"Sure," she responded, somewhat sullenly.

Closing the door behind him, he walked further into the room, closer to Faith. She stepped back. Tilting his head as he looked at her, he took two steps closer. Her feet two steps back.

"Why didn't you pick up my calls yesterday and today," he asked.

"I've been busy. Plus, if I hadn't picked up your calls, how am I still watching Madison tonight?" she hissed.

Giving her a look of frustration, he ran his hand down his face, "What's wrong with you, Faith? Why are you acting like this?" Looking at her with something akin to hurt in his eyes, his voice was low as he asked her, "What's going on with us? You said you were okay with this."

Teeth clenched, she glared at him in frustration, "I am," she ground out. Glancing into the living room, she yelled out in a happy tone of voice, "I'll go get you some dinner, honey. Keep on watching your show."

"Okay," Madison yelled back over her shoulder.

Walking into the kitchen, she knew Cooper would be following. How in the hell would she answer his question? Give him the truth? Hell, no. Avoidance? Absolutely!

"What do you mean, Cooper? How am I acting exactly? You thanked me for watching Madison. I said sure. What else is there to say?" She knew exactly why she was behaving standoffish. Her feelings were hurt that Cooper had a date. It had solidified her initial thought that the other weekend had been a fluke. A momentary lapse in judgement.

And honestly, knowing that she had just been a fill-in really sucked. Even after they had spoken a few days ago, here he was, standing in here in her kitchen about to go on a date.

Hands in his pockets, Cooper stood staring at her, probably trying to figure out what the hell to say next. Eyes blazing fire in her direction, she saw his firm jaw working overtime and knew he was grinding his back teeth. Not a stupid man, she was positive Cooper knew exactly what was bothering her.

Unwilling to give him the satisfaction of seeing how hurt she really was, she stood firm and didn't say a word. It would be a cold day in hell before she told him what was really wrong. Let him stew in his own juices. Two could play this game.

"Come on, Faith. That 'sure' didn't sound quite right," he said, finally breaking the silent standoff. Taking one step further into the kitchen, he continued, "Are you sure you're okay with watching Madison tonight? This date is just a formality. It won't mean anything. Plus, you said for me to go!" With his voice raised, he stopped and lowered his head. She watched him take a few breaths, "I won't be that long. When I get back, we're going to talk about this. About us. I don't like this. This isn't us."

"Cooper, I told you that I would watch her." Getting annoyed now, her voice had a hint of steel, "Just leave, Cooper. Go out on your date. I'm sure she's waiting for you."

"Yeah, I guess I had better. You know, this was scheduled more than three weeks ago. It was just hard to cancel on her this late in the game. You understand that right, Faith?" His voice implored her to listen.

Unfortunately, Faith wasn't in the mood to be forgiving tonight.

Then again, what right did she have to be upset with him? No promises had been made between the two of them. No declarations of love had been whispered into the night. They were just two people who enjoyed each other's company and maybe had some slight sexual attraction. It wasn't his fault that Faith found herself falling in love with a man who considered her a substitute. And a poor one at that.

"Cooper, don't worry about it. Go on your hot date." Briefly looking down at her chosen attire for the evening, then over at him, she took a deep breath, "No, seriously, I'm fine. I'll hang out with Madison and we'll do water paints, eat creamy mac and cheese, and probably make cupcakes. My life of glamour and excitement."

"I think that sounds like an amazing night," he said while removing his hands from his pocket and taking a few more steps into the kitchen. Closer to her, yet again.

"Riiiggghhht. Which is why you're headed into the city for a swanky dinner with your hot date and I'm here in old gray sweatpants," she responded.

"Didn't you have a hot date just over a month ago? At least I'm telling you where I'm going," he said with anger lacing his voice.

Frustration seemed to pour off of him and she was momentarily stunned. She watched as he closed his eyes for a second. When they opened, he was calm again and he gave her a brief smile. His eyes then roamed over her body, taking her in from head to toe, "I think you look beautiful, Faith. You always do, no matter what you have on. I like you just the way you are."

Although she shouldn't be, Faith was hurt by his words. Now he was just being cruel. What was all that anger about just a few minutes ago? Was he trying to make her crazy with his back-and-forth? One minute he was hot, the next cold.

Shaking her head to clear away the unintended impact of his words, she busied herself by putting dinner on a plate for her and Madison. "I'm fine. Leave, Cooper."

Her back was turned to him, so when his voice sounded in her ear, she jumped. "I should be back around eleven o'clock tonight. Is that too late for you?"

How the hell had he gotten so close to her so quickly? His face was inches away from hers and she was tempted to throw caution to the wind and capture his lips in a kiss. Right then and there. "N-No, I'll be here," she responded, cringing inside at the breathless tone of her voice. "Aren't I always here when you need me?"

His eyes became serious as he continued to stare at her. Heat began to spread through her body as the memory of last week entered her mind. Could he see how much she wanted him? Was her desire and need for him written all over her face?

"Yes, you are," his deep voice was low and raspy as he seemed to speak to her soul. Raising one hand to cup her cheek, he leaned in slowly.

Bracing herself, Faith's eyes began to close as she waited for the touch of his lips on hers. Oh gawd, she needed this so much.

"Which is why I'm so happy we're friends," he said as his lips brushed her cheek, just centimeters from her mouth. Almost instinctively, her head turned in his direction, but he pulled away. Stepping back, he had a look on his face that she couldn't decipher.

What? Her eyes opened in disbelief.

Cooper looked at his watch, "Alright, love, I have to get going. I'll be back in a few hours." As Cooper walked away, her eyes began to well with tears. She heard Madison's squeal as she said goodbye to him.

"Bye, Faith! I'm locking the front door."

Words failed her. What the hell was wrong with her? The man was clearly not feeling the same things she was. Tears began to fall down her face as she considered everything that happened.

How could he go out on a date with someone else? With everything they had done together. All of the late nights and weekends, the cooking for each other, the phone calls at night before bed, the calls in the middle of the day just to talk. Did it mean nothing to him?

She wondered what his date looked like. Did she have the strawberry blonde hair and green eyes reminiscent of his wife? Was he still focused on finding a woman that looked like the one he had lost? Never once did she consider that maybe his date resembled her. No, Faith was not his ideal, which pissed her off even more, while her crying became even more intense.

Why was she wasting her time with this? This was completely ridiculous. No man had ever defined her or caused her to doubt her own appeal. He was right, they were friends.

Their playful, flirty banter, was just that. Nothing more and she would do well to remember that next time. For a while, she had hoped it would be more, but he seemed to look right through her. At times, she wanted to kiss him and smack him at the same time, forcing him to see her and recognize that the woman standing in front of him was all he needed.

∞ ∞ ∞ ∞ ∞

Cooper didn't belong here. Wanting nothing more than to be at home with Faith and Madison, he took a bite of his steak and tuned in to what his date was saying.

"You're so smart. Why did you go into the military?"

"Excuse me?" Did he just hear her right?

Taking another bite of her salad, she took a sip of water, and had the unmitigated gall to ask again, "Well, I'm just wondering why you would go into the military. You have a degree, you're a CFO at a large company. Just seems odd."

Patting his mouth with his cloth napkin, he looked at her across the table and again wondered what the hell he was doing. Simply looking at her, she was everything he thought he wanted. Once upon a time. Her light brown hair had streaks of blonde throughout. Hazel eyes stared at him under thick lashes, and her lips bore a permanent pout. Tall and thin, her curves were minimal, just as he had always liked. Before Faith.

"I haven't always been a CFO," he responded tightly.

"Well, I know that. But you had other options, right? She continued to press.

"Actually, no, I didn't. The military was my lifeline. I was given a choice. Jail or military. I chose the military." Why was he even telling her this? It was time to leave.

Just at that moment, the waiter came over to take their plates, "Would you like to see our dessert menu?"

"No." Rude, maybe. But he'd had enough.

"Yes, sir. Coffee for the lady?"

"Yes, a cappuccino, please. You don't mind, do you, Cooper?"

Her saccharine sweet voice had begun to grate on his nerves and he felt a headache beginning to form behind his eyes.

"No, of course I don't mind. I'll have a double espresso," he gave the order to the waiter, praying the drinks would come soon.

After another twenty minutes in her presence, he had reached his limit. Parting ways outside of the restaurant after paying the check, he tried to let her down easy.

"Would you like to come by my place for a nightcap?" Resting her hand on his chest, she pressed closer to him.

"No, thanks. I need to get home," he said while pulling her hands away from him. Even her perfume was starting to stink. Damn, he needed to get the hell away from her. Whatever made him think this was a good idea? There was no way in hell he would see her again. She was nothing like Heather and she didn't even come close to Faith.

Faith.

Fuck! What was he thinking? "It was nice Liz, but I need to leave. Take care of yourself." And with those parting words, he turned and walked to his car. He was going home to the woman he truly wanted to be with.

Getting into his truck and driving back to his neighborhood, he wondered if Faith really gave a fuck that he had been out on a date with another woman. Wouldn't it be some shit if she did, especially after what she had pulled a few weeks ago? She may have thought he had forgotten, but he hadn't. Every word she said about the guy, every nuance of her voice as she spoke about their date, every word she had used to describe him, was burned into his brain.

Tonight was an attempt to see if he could move on with another woman. Could what he was feeling for Faith be replicated with someone else? He wasn't dumb. Cooper knew that because they had grown so close, his feelings for her would eventually become muddled. Maybe his attraction to her wasn't real after all. It felt wrong to even think that way. It seemed wrong to question Faith's feelings for him. Standing so close to her tonight at her home, the tears in her eyes had not gone unnoticed. At the moment, he was committed to his path. If he was going to give his life to her, his love, he needed there to be no doubts. For either of them.

There had been several dates, and nightcaps, with women before he had met her. Before they had become so close and he was no longer willing to hide from the intensity of his feelings for her. Afterward, there had been no one serious and the occasional happy hour with his work colleagues or friendly outings had been okay. Always aware of the plans he had with Faith and Madison, he had always kept the balance and kept any hint of "another woman" away from Faith. That is, until this stupid move tonight. Hitting the steering wheel with the palm of his hand, he knew he had been a fool to do this.

Even when he went out with someone that he enjoyed spending time with before he met Faith, if he saw them after she had come into his life, it wasn't the same. The spark was gone. Each time a nightcap was offered, he turned it down. He would see the light in their eyes dim at the realization that he was no longer interested.

How the hell was he going to handle this? Without realizing what he was doing, he began to speak to Heather, as he would often do when dealing with a dilcmma.

"I just don't know what to do about Faith. She drives me crazy sometimes. And she never listens to me," he spoke into the air. "Madison loves her, though. I know she does. And Faith loves our daughter just as much."

If he listened close enough, he could almost hear his wife's laugh as he shared the details of his life with her. His life that he continued to live without her by his side. It felt good to talk to her, but he knew this too was coming to an end. It had almost broken him when he had lost Heather and holding on to her was all he knew to do. The thought of loving Faith, of building a life with her, and maybe losing her one day, scared the shit out of him.

Being in the military had taught him that life could be snuffed out in the blink of an eye. Hell, he had learned that lesson a long time ago. No one looking at him, not even his parents, would have a clue about how things were so many years ago. He hadn't been lying to Liz when he told her that he had received an ultimatum. Luckily, his dad had been friends with some cops and they had put in a good word for him when he had been caught selling drugs and running with a group of kids that were headed nowhere fast.

Whether it was his need to rebel or there was just something in him that caused him to turn to the dark side, he wasn't sure. All he knew was that it was time for him to turn things around. Seeing his mother cry broke his heart. Hearing his father beat himself up for not being good enough, tore him up. His parents had done all they could to keep him on the straight and narrow. The choices had been his.

When faced with a decision to do something different or stay on a course that would lead him down a path to more criminal activity, or even death, he chose wisely. Taking his first leap of faith, he chose the military. And he never looked back.

Continuing his conversation with his dead wife, he smiled ruefully into the empty space, "Madison is just like you, with a little touch of me. When she loves, she loves hard. And, sweetheart, she loves Faith." His voice began to choke up as he continued, "I know it wouldn't have been possible if you were alive, but I wish you could meet Faith. I think you would like her. The two of you are polar opposites, but I see the same qualities in her that I saw in you. My love for you won't go away, but I need Faith in my life. I can't let her go and if she'll have me, I won't ever leave her again."

Going silent, he let the impact of his words sink in. He had never compared any other woman to his wife. For him to feel comfortable speaking the words, made something in his heart tighten, even as his brain tried to purge the thought.

Damn, he was fucked.

Chapter Ten

Pulling up to his home, he saw that all of the lights at Faith's house were out. His truck's digital display showed a quarter after ten, so it was still quite early. Thinking that they must be sleeping, he was tempted to let them be. Changing his mind at the thought of Faith thinking he was still out with another woman, he altered his steps and walked up to her home.

Knocking lightly, it took only a few seconds for Faith to arrive at the front door. As soon as she opened the door, she put one finger up to her mouth and stepped back, allowing space for him to walk in.

"You're back early," she said as they stood in the entrance.

"Yeah, my night ended early. I wanted to get back home to my girls," he said.

"Your girls? Cooper, you only have one daughter," she smiled at him as she said it, but her eyes reflected confusion, and dare he say it, hope.

"I know exactly what I meant, Faith," he growled as he stepped closer to her. "You haven't asked me how my date went," he whispered as he bent his head low and whispered in her ear, "Why would I? I'm sure it was fine," she said as she folded her arms. A surefire sign that she was trying to close herself off from him. Not tonight. He needed her to understand.

"Did it escape your attention that I'm home early?" he asked.

Turning her back to him, she muttered, "Yes, I noticed. But it doesn't matter."

Walking up behind her, he pressed his body against hers and instantly became hard. Seconds later, he felt her lean back against him and he felt that all was right in the world.

"Why doesn't it matter, Faith? I'm home now. Where I belong," he responded. The plea for understanding was laced within every word.

After a pause, she answered, "Because you left in the first place." Turning her head to the side, he felt her take a few deep breaths and then freeze. Suddenly, she pulled back, her face screwed up in disgust.

"You stink."

Surprised by her words, it took him a minute to understand what she was saying, "Faith…" he began, but her hand came up to stop him.

"No, Cooper, I don't want to hear it. It's not my business. You're free to do whatever you want, with whomever you want," her voice cracked as she was finishing and it tore at him.

"Are you even going to let me explain?" Now he was getting angry. Did she really think he would leave the arms of another woman and come to her? Touch her?

"No," she responded as he stared at her in shock. "Again, not my issue." Backing away from him, she got to the door of the room where Madison was sleeping. "Madison can stay here with me tonight. We're making blueberry pancakes in the morning. If you want breakfast."

"Faith, are you serious right now," he asked as she stood her ground. She was the most stubborn, opinionated, maddening woman he had ever met.

"Keep your voice down Cooper!" Closing the doors leading to the family room where Madison was sleeping, she turned back to him and simply stood here.

God, he wanted to make love to her so fucking bad right now, but she would probably slap him if he approached her. His brain may be saying one thing, but his throbbing cock was saying another. No other woman would do for him. Ever. Now his job was to help her see it.

"Fine, I'm leaving. But before I go," he said as he walked toward her. He was positive she was expecting him to walk in and kiss Madison good night. She was sorely mistaken. This was about him and her.

Striding up to her, he grabbed her arm, not hard, but with enough pull that she came forward, stumbling into him.

"Cooper, what are you doing?"

"I'm saying goodnight," he responded. His hands came up and grabbed her face as his head tilted down, his lips pressing into hers.

Her mouth opened in a gasp of surprise and he took the opportunity to deepen the kiss, his tongue gliding into her mouth, seeking out hers. The moan that released from her almost made him cum on the spot. This...fucking...woman. One word popped up in his head. Mine!

Releasing his hands from her face, he slid them down her body to her thighs. In one strong motion, he lifted her up, placing her hot core right over where his cock lay. Hands grabbing her under the ass, he continued kissing, his tongue dueling with hers. All he could think was that she tasted like heaven. Why had he waited so long?

Almost to the brink of losing control, all he wanted to do was sink inside of her until he couldn't tell where he ended and she began. Her moans continued to reach his ears as they kissed deeply. His hands began to press her ass closer as he ground his hips into her. All he could think of was that they both needed to be naked, and his cock should be buried to the hilt inside of her.

Their mouths separated for a moment and he began kissing her neck, just below her ear. Ragged breath and low whimpers were all he could here. And then she said the words that made his world tilt on its axis.

"Cooper, please," she begged.

For what, he wasn't sure. But at this moment, he would give her anything in his power. Lifting his head, he looked into her eyes and saw raw passion. He was positive that his eyes reflected the same.

"Baby, I need you. Faith, please baby, don't deny me." His voice sounded foreign to him.

"I would nev –," she was in the middle of speaking when they both heard a sound come from the room where Madison was sleeping.

"Faith?" The little voice echoed through the house. It served to jolt both of them out of their sexual frenzy. Hands pushing against him, Faith squirmed out of his arms, forcing him to release her. Her legs unwrapped from his waist and her feet hit the ground. Looking at him with uncertainty in her eyes, she skirted around him and left him standing there panting with barely unleashed desire.

"I'm coming, honey," she called out to his little girl as she walked away.

Breathing deeply, Cooper tried to rein in his emotions. They were on the verge of having sex in the middle of her foyer. His daughter just in the next room over. Calming down to the point where he could move with some semblance of normalcy, he stood up straight and adjusted his pants, moving his hardness out of the way so that it wasn't as noticeable. Yeah, right. With how he was feeling right now, that wasn't going to work very well.

Faith stepped back out of the family room and walked toward him. Looking down at her, he knew that their moment of passion had passed. Whatever had flared up between them just moments ago had calmed down to a low simmer.

"She's asleep again. I think she just turned over and noticed that I wasn't in the room with her," she said. "She's back asleep now."

"Do you want me to go?" He knew what he wanted her to say, but it was her choice.

"No. I don't," she admitted, a sexy smile coming over her face as she glanced down at the still noticeable bulge in his pants.

"Oh thank God, let's go—," she interrupted before he could finish.

"But, I think you should. We need to think about this Cooper. I'm not sure if you're even ready for this."

"Why would you say that? I just showed you that I'm more than ready to be with you," he said, confused by what she was saying.

Looking away briefly, she turned back to him, her gaze strong and sure, "Have you gotten over Heather?"

Startled by her question, he said the first thing that came into his mind, "What the hell does my wife have anything to do with this?"

"Oh, Cooper, don't you see? She has everything to do with this." Pausing for a moment and walking further away from the room where Madison slept and closer to him. "Answer me this. Are you still married?"

"Faith, that is unfair. Don't use my wife to push me away," he said, his voice filled with frustration.

"I don't have to. You just did."

About to reach out to her, he stilled. In that moment, clarity hit him like a lightning bolt and he knew exactly what was wrong. Faith had asked him about Heather and he had responded in present-tense, not past. His libido may be ready to move on, but unconsciously, he considered himself still married.

"Faith, this night is not ending like I had planned." Placing both hands on his hips, he dipped his head low. How the hell was he supposed to fight this? Couldn't she understand how difficult this was for him?

"I know it didn't. But, it ended the way it was supposed to." Opening the door for him, she stood there waiting, "Go home, Cooper. Breakfast will be ready at ten in the morning. We'll be here waiting for you when you decide to join us."

Knowing when he was defeated and that it was best to pull back and regroup, Cooper walked to the open door. Stopping just in front of her, he cupped her face with one of his hands. Her eyes closed as she pressed closer into his warm palm, her lips brushing a light kiss against his skin. It had been such a stupid slip, but to Faith, he knew it was the one thing holding them apart.

"Really, Cooper, it's okay. You'll know when it's time."

"I know that I'm ready now, Faith. I didn't mean it the way it sounded. You have to see that. Now that I've found you, I'm not willing to let you go so easily," the words sounded strained.

Her eyes glistened as she looked up at him, "I'll be here. But for now, let's slow down. Can we do that?"

"Do I have a choice?" He had completely fucked this up and now he had to pay the price.

"Not really. Good night, Cooper," she smiled at him.

"Night, baby." Stepping out of the door, he turned as she closed it. Something caused him to pause before he walked away. Soon after he heard the locks engage, he heard a sound come through the door. Unsure of what it was at first, he leaned closer, pressing his ear to the wood. There it was again.

He felt his breath catch as he recognized the sound. Crying.

Faith was crying on the other side of the door and it was all because of him. Resting his forehead on the door, he was unable to move. There was no way he could leave her now. Not with that sound coming through the door and piercing his heart like a knife. Knowing that she's hurting on the other side of the door, and trying to hide it from him, slayed him.

Making a decision, he knocked softly on the door. With her being right on the other side, he knew she would hear it. When a few seconds passed, but no more crying could be heard, he knocked softly again. He soon heard the locks and then the door opened.

One look at her face and he knew this had been the right decision. Stepping inside, his large frame caused her to step back as he entered her home again. "Baby, why are you doing this? Please, Faith, don't cry."

Gathering her in his arms, he held her while he felt tiny tremors course through her body, "I'm not going anywhere. I know you think I'm not over Heather. And while right now is not the time to talk about that, I will prove to you that all I need, all I want, is you. But tonight, is all about you. I refuse to walk away from this house and leave you. My place is here, with you and Madison."

"I don't want her to find us in my bed, Cooper. That would confuse her too much," she responded in a watery voice.

"Fine, then let's sleep on the big couch in the other room. She's already on the small one and you were going to sleep in the room with her anyway." His back would hurt like hell and he would probably be awake all night, but it would be worth it. Any other time, maybe he would force the issue of lying on a comfortable mattress—but tonight was not that moment. If she wanted them to sleep on the couch, that's what he would do.

Lifting her head, she wiped her eyes, "I probably look a mess."

Cupping her face with his hands, he lifted her head up so that he could look directly into her eyes, "You look beautiful. Never doubt it."

“You’re a liar, Mr. Branson, but I’ll take it. Okay, let me go get some blankets. I even think I have some of your shorts and a t-shirt over here.”

“I’ll be right here, Faith,” he said as she walked away. He meant every word.

∞ ∞ ∞ ∞ ∞

Faith’s eyes opened to the sunlight. Her face was pressed against a warm body, her mouth open. One of her arms was wrapped around his waist, her hand splayed on his back. Cooper’s leg was in between hers and her top leg was curled around his thigh. Slowly peeling herself away from him, she could feel herself blush at the scene.

Lifting her eyes to Cooper’s face, she admired his profile for a few minutes. They had never slept this closely before. Unwrapping her arm from his back, she felt him shift and stilled. Peeking over her shoulder, she made sure that Madison was still sleeping. All she needed was for the little girl to wake up and see her daddy and Ms. Faith in a compromising position.

Turning back to Cooper, his eyes were still closed and his breathing even. Taking the opportunity in front of her, she ran her fingertips along his jaw in a feather-soft touch. In sleep, he looked so peaceful. You wouldn’t know that inside was a sleeping lion.

Not only had he been trained to take a life in a matter of seconds, but he had done so in the heat of battle. The unseen scars were as much a part of him as the visible ones that crisscrossed his bare chest and arms. He tried to hide that side of him, but she knew better. Growing up in a neighborhood where you had to learn how to handle yourself on a daily basis, where kids saw and experienced way too much, she knew the look of someone trying to hide their pain away from everyone.

Being strong was all he knew. She understood that. She accepted that. After last night, with what almost happened between them, she knew there had to be some changes.

Extricating her limbs from his, she slid from the couch to the floor like a slinky. Almost laughing out loud at the picture she made, she lay there for a few minutes trying to stay quiet. As long as Madison stayed asleep until she got up off of the floor that was all she needed. Getting up after a few minutes, she crept quietly out of the room, leaving the two people who held her heart sleeping peacefully.

After taking a quick shower and putting on clean clothes, she made her way into the kitchen and started pulling out the ingredients for their breakfast. Mind wandering as she moved around her kitchen, she thought back to last night.

God, that man made her forget who she was. When he knocked on her door the first time, she saw the time, but hadn't given it much thought. Not until he came in all caveman style, making her panties wet and driving her crazy with his tongue and hands. If it hadn't been for Madison calling out her name, who knows where they would have ended up.

Remembering the thickness of his cock rubbing at her center as they kissed, she felt her body start to respond to the memory of how good it felt. So powerful and strong, she gasped again as she remembered how he picked her up as if she weighed nothing. There was such power in his body, but he kept it hidden behind the facade of a carefree dad, who just so happened to wear a suit every day. If she had anything to say about it, she would have that man in her bed soon. And once there, she would be damned if he would leave.

This was her moment. It would finally be her chance to find happiness, and she couldn't wait.

Picking up the sounds of movement in the other room, she refocused on the task at hand. Making breakfast for the man she loved and the little girl that had stolen her heart.

∞ ∞ ∞ ∞ ∞

"Daddy, Daddy! You had a sleepover with me and Ms. Faith!"

Cooper's eyes came open just as his daughter launched herself onto his chest. "Oomph!" Wincing a little in pain as she landed on top of him, "Morning, princess."

"We made pancakes and bacon and cheesy eggs. Ms. Faith said that cheesy eggs are the best, so I'm going to have a whole bunch," her chatter continued even as Cooper lifted up from lying prone on the couch.

Damn, his back hurt like a motherfucker. Clearly he had gotten soft after being out of the military for so long. There were nights that he and his team had slept on the hard ground with little more than their rucksack as a pillow. He stretched his neck and twisted his back to loosen up the kinks. "Okay, honey, where's Ms. Faith?"

"She's in the kitchen. She told me to come wake you up, so I did," she seemed proud that she could contribute. “Come on, Daddy. You have five minutes. Ms. Faith said.”

“Okay, I’m getting up now. I’ll be there in two minutes. How does that sound?”

“I’ll go tell her,” she said as she turned tail and ran back to the kitchen.

Lifting up from the couch, he stretched and walked to the guest bathroom. Thank goodness Faith was a smart girl. He was lucky that she had some of his clothes over here from their many visits and outings. Plus, she kept a cadre of toothbrushes for guests to use. Oh yeah, that woman of his was the real deal.

His woman? Yeah, she was. That became true the moment he laid eyes on her. It just took his brain and heart time to catch up.

As he walked into the kitchen, he heard their voices raised in song, singing one of those catchy tunes playing on the radio lately. Smiling at their antics as they set the table and as Faith brought over the hot food on platters. Next came the orange juice and coffee for them, and strawberry milk for Madison.

Faith was the first one to see him, “Good morning, Cooper. Hungry?”

“Starving,” he said while eyeing her, instead of the food on the table. Grinning at her like a wolf eyeing a tasty treat, he watched her eyes widen as she picked up on what he was saying. Mouthing, “soon baby,” in her direction, he turned to the table and saw Madison standing there looking so proud. “Everything looks really good. Did you help make this, munchkin?”

"I sure did, Daddy. I helped with the pancakes. Can you tell?"

Looking intently at the fluffy blueberry filled flapjacks, he exclaimed, "I sure can! Great job, honey."

All of them sat down, with Faith saying grace. That done, they all dug into the food. Faith made Madison's plate, only giving her a silver dollar size pancake, a small scoop of cheesy eggs, and one slice of bacon.

"How did you sleep," he asked her once they had settled in to eat.

"It was wonderful, actually," she responded after taking a drink of juice. "I woke up before both of you and started getting everything ready." She eyed Madison and he picked up the hint that his little girl had not seen them lying together on the couch wrapped in each other's arms.

"Ah, well, then I'm glad. So, what's on tap for the day?"

"I have a little bit of work to do and some laundry," Faith responded.

"Actually, I need to make a trip to see Heather's parents. I forgot that I promised them that Madison and I would see them today." Once he finished, he looked up at Faith's face. He hadn't forgotten their conversation last night and he was hoping she would understand that there was a difference in thinking of himself as married to someone who had passed, and keeping his daughter connected to both sides of her family. Maintaining balance for Madison was important.

"Faith—," he began.

"No, it's fine Cooper. I really do understand. This is important, for both you and Madison." Her tentative smile reminded him that she had not forgotten their conversation, either. "Really. I understand. Don't worry about it."

"Ms. Faith, do you want to come with me to see my Mimi and Papi?" Out of the mouths of babes, Cooper almost cringed at the implications of taking Faith to his in-laws house.

"No, sweetie, not this time. I think this is a special day for you and your daddy." Faith turned to him and gave a slight smile. "But I'll be here when you get back, okay?"

"Okay."

Cooper released a breath he didn't realize he was holding. He definitely needed to deal with this. If he were ready to move on with life, his in-laws—no, his daughter's grandparents, would just have to understand.

Chapter Eleven

Damn, he was tired. His shoulders were tight and sore, the muscles screaming for relief. Stress was bearing down on him from all levels and there seemed to be no escape. His days were long and they weren't getting any easier. Plus, after his visit to his in-laws on Sunday, they had been calling him nonstop. Before he had a chance to explain to them about how things were changing with Faith, Madison had opened the floodgates.

"Mimi, me and daddy had a sleepover with Ms. Faith. And then we cooked breakfast and daddy said he could tell which ones I made and which ones Ms. Faith made," she said innocently, unknowingly broaching a subject he hadn't been sure he was ready to have at that moment, Madison went back to playing with her blocks.

Heather's parents had stared at him in shock. His father-in-law looked at him for a few seconds, then glanced over at Heather's mother and shook his head no. When Cooper looked at his mother-in-law, her lips were pursed in anger and her eyes had filled with tears.

What an uncomfortable conversation that had been. While Madison was outside playing with her grandfather on her swing set in their backyard, his mother-in-law had cornered him in the kitchen.

"Really, Cooper! What were you thinking? You slept with another woman with my granddaughter in the house?" Blinking back tears, she continued, "What would Heather think?"

That's what hurt him the most. Not sure what Heather would think, he was simply trying to do what was best. For him and Madison. After all the years they had been together, he knew his wife and he was positive that she could find no fault in what he had done. Not once had he disrespected her, or her memory. If anything, his actions had kept her memory alive and well, probably to his own detriment.

Suffice it to say, that had not been a pleasant visit. While he explained the situation, which he didn't really have to do in the first place, he knew that they still wondered if by moving on with Faith, he would forget about Heather. How could he? For the rest of his life, he would see her reflected in the eyes of his daughter.

Opening the back door of the vehicle, he unbuckled his little angel from her booster seat and helped her exit the truck. Once he placed her on the ground, he reached in for her pink, princess themed backpack. Turning back to his daughter, a smile graced his face as he watched her twirl around, her dress ballooning in the air, "Alright, Madison, let's head in. Do you want spaghetti or meatloaf tonight?"

Pausing in place, she put her hands on her hips and tilted her head as if in deep thought, "Um, meatloaf, Daddy." Answer given, she reached her arms up for him to lift her. Smiling down at the miniature image of his wife, he knew that she trusted that he would always be there for her and heaven help him, he hoped she never had to learn otherwise.

"Okay, honey. You got it. How was school today?" Making idle chatter as he held his little girl in his arms, he closed the car door with his foot, and walked to the front door. Walking up the front steps, he placed his daughter on the ground.

Fumbling in his pocket, he pulled out his keys so that he could unlock the door. All the while, his daughter had kept up her running commentary about her friends. It was amazing that someone so small could talk so much.

Thank goodness he had some vacation planned in the next few days. He needed a break from the craziness of this week. Four days of relaxation and hanging out with his daughter seemed like the right answer. Things were becoming even more hectic at work lately and being the head of finance at a medium sized marketing firm in Northern Virginia brought its own level of strain. This weekend, it would be all about him and his daughter, having fun.

Hearing Faith's car pull into her driveway, he paused for a moment. Slowing down his efforts to enter his home before she stepped out of her car, he turned his body so that he was facing the direction of her home. It wasn't very often that they both arrived home at the same time and he was somewhat surprised to see her. But now that she was here, his night was looking much better.

Madison's loud yelling pulled him away from his internal thoughts.

"Daddy! It's Ms. Faith! I want to go see her."

Looking down at his little girl pulling at his suit jacket, he smiled. "Yes, honey. Okay, let me get the door open and put our stuff down. Then we can go say hi to Faith. Okay?"

Looking across the yard, he watched his woman step out of her car and pull her briefcase out. It seemed as if she were in a world of her own and hadn't even seen them. Just as she was closing the door and about to make her way into the house, Madison yelled out to her, "Ms. Faith! Come here!"

Laughing slightly at her demanding tone, Cooper tried to rein in his four-year old spitfire. "Honey, you know that's not how you talk to Ms. Faith. You have to ask her nicely."

"But why, Daddy? I want to see her." She began jumping up down in excitement. Looking across the yard, he noticed that Faith had stopped to look at them as well. A huge smile split her face as she took in the sight of his daughter anxiously waiting to see her.

Placing her briefcase on the hood of her car, she slung her purse over her shoulder and began taking steps toward them. At the same time, Madison took off like a bolt of lightning across the grassy expanse between their two houses.

As soon as she was close enough, Madison launched herself toward Faith, arms spread wide and a grin bigger than the moon in the sky. Luckily, Faith had anticipated this and was able to bend down and position her body and open her arms, ready to catch the little girl as she flew into her arms.

Faith kissed the little girl's cheeks as she greeted her, "Hey there, princess. How was school today?"

Catching her gaze as she listened to his daughter talk a mile a minute, he noticed that Faith looked a bit more tired today than usual. Instantly, he became concerned. Seeing that look on her face was not something he enjoyed. Not at all. Giving her a questioning look as their eyes met over his daughter's head, he mouthed the words, "Everything okay?"

Faith began nodding her head slowly up-and-down, as if to say that she was fine. But then she changed motions and began shaking her head back and forth, letting him know that his instincts had been right. Something was definitely wrong. Almost stepping in to remove his daughter from her arms, she mouthed back to him, "I'm fine."

She then turned her attention back to his daughter as they stood in the yard in between the two homes, the sun setting in the background and a light breeze flowing through the air. At that moment, Cooper knew that things had changed forever. That he was ready to let go. That building a life with the woman standing across from him was what he wanted most in this world.

His hands itched to reach out and touch her, to give her comfort. Suddenly, he had the feeling that he wanted to make love to her tonight. Feeling her move underneath him, above him, or even beside was all he could think about.

Looking at the two of them standing there together, he got a sudden image of this being his everyday life. Coming home from work with Faith and Madison greeting him as he exited the car. Something twisted inside of him and he quickly realized that this is what he had been feeling all along, but refusing to accept.

It was more than just a physical attraction to the beautiful, dark-skinned, curvy woman standing only feet away from him. It was so much more than that, and he had been blind not to have seen it earlier. She was the type of woman he and Madison needed in their lives. Only problem was, he wasn't sure if he had blown it.

Examining his own behavior lately and why she had been so upset on Sunday during breakfast, he finally saw himself through her eyes. Every word out of his mouth was focused on what he and Heather had together. How he and Heather had lived their life. All of the things he did to keep her memory alive, not only for Madison, but for himself.

He had been a fool. Honoring Heather didn't prevent him from loving again. It would just be a different kind of love, because he was now a different man. But it would be no less powerful and all-consuming. Faith was a different woman and her love for him came in a different package. There was no shame in that.

Comparing her to Heather or injecting his late-wife into every facet of the life they had built together, even before he realized that his feelings had changed, had not been fair. To himself or to Faith. No woman would want that thrown in their face at every turn. He had been a very selfish man to the woman he loved. Never again.

He had to fix the damage he had already done. Nothing would get in the way of him making things right with Faith. If he had to spend the next fifty years showing her just how much he wanted—needed her by his side, then that's what he would do.

Cooper made up his mind while standing in their front yard. Faith would be his for life. From this day forward, all his efforts would go to proving to her how much she meant to him.

Glancing at his watch, he saw that it was getting close to dinnertime. He needed to get his ladies in the house. Walking past them, he went over to her car and picked up her briefcase. "Come on, you two. It's dinner time and you both need to eat."

At Faith's look, he knew she was going to try and back out and go home. "No, Love, you're coming with us. Tonight is my night to feed you. You two can finish your conversation in the house."

∞ ∞ ∞ ∞ ∞

Faith's heart was beating so fast, she would swear it was about to burst out of her chest. Did she just hear Cooper call her love? After the ups and downs of the last few weeks, she was hesitant to jump to any conclusions about what that actually meant. Positive she was hearing things, she almost asked him to repeat what he said, but chose to let it go. Still shocked at her reaction to that one word coming from his lips, if he had turned to look in her direction, he would have seen the questioning look across her features, which surely would have made him inquire into what had caused it.

Cooper and Madison had returned late on Sunday, so they only had the chance for a quick call that night. All he would say about the visit was that it had been “tough”. His words. They still hadn’t spoken in detail about his visit to his in-laws house, but she expected that conversation to take place tonight. To deny that she was somewhat nervous about what happened, would be the understatement of the year.

They had planned to see each other both Monday and Tuesday, just to catch up and talk. Work had been keeping her busy the last couple of nights and it had always been too late for them to see each other. Tonight was the first time they had both arrived home at the same time. Both early enough to see each other and spend some significant time with each other.

With one-ear, she listened to the litany of daily preschool adventures from Madison. As she looked over at Cooper, he was carrying her belongings as if it were the most natural thing in the world. Watching him as he walked in front of them, leading the way to front door of his home, she could not prevent that small ray of hope that flared in her chest. With everything in her, she wanted to believe that the uncertainty was over. That he finally realized that she was here for him. Wanted to be with him.

No matter how much she wanted to, she would no longer push him to move past Heather. That had to be his choice. Smiling at the little girl in her arms, she thought about the impact on Madison if she tried to erase her mother from her father's memory. They had a full life together. Had been through trials and tribulations that she and Cooper may never experience. If she stayed stuck on this path, it would come back to haunt her in the future. That wasn't the type of person she was, and she knew it.

It was time for her let things move naturally. No more pressing or pushing, but she would make her desires known. After that, the ball would be in his court. Either he wanted her in his life, or he didn't. No more half-stepping. She deserved better.

Walking through the front door of the house into the foyer, she felt Madison lay her head on her shoulder and wrap her arms around her neck. She knew what that meant.

"Uh oh, the octopus has come out to play," Cooper commented as he shut the door behind them.

"Yeah, but that's okay. I love it," she responded as she kissed the little girl's forehead. Her skin was so soft. Cradling her little body in her arms, Faith couldn't think of anything sweeter than having Madison's trust.

Madison had a tendency to transform herself into an octopus when she wanted Faith to spend time with her, which mainly consisted of Faith just holding her in her arms. Kicking off her low pumps and pushing them to the side of the wall next to multiple pairs of shoes thrown about by Cooper and Madison, she raised one hand to rub along her tiny back.

"Hey, baby girl, want to sit with me while your dad gets dinner started," although she asked the question, this was just a formality. A part of the game they played.

If Faith presented the idea first, it was then her idea and not Madison's. That tended to make for an easier transition and the little girl relaxed a little faster. For such a young child, she had been through so much. Faith knew this and never hesitated to provide what she could to help with her continued adjustment.

Looking up at her with those beautiful blue eyes that she now understood were so much like her mother's, despite the color, Madison continued their little game. "Yes, Ms. Faith, I can keep you company. Don't you want to watch the movie about the princess and she turns into a frog and then she kisses the prince?"

By now, her arms had come from around Faith's neck and her little hands were cradling Faith's face. Little imp that she was, her eyes gave Faith a long look imploring her to play along. "You know, honey,

I think I do. I haven't seen that movie in almost a full week and it's my most favorite one."

Feeling Cooper's gaze on the two of them, she fought the urge to turn around and look at him. Fear that her own longing for the man himself would come through, she tried to focus her attention solely on his little girl. This shyness around him was new. They hadn't been shy or reserved around each other since that first day.

But things had changed so much and she didn't think they could ever go back to the way they were before the last few weeks. Knowing that it was childish to try and avoid eye contact, she tried to gather her nerves. Standing in the middle of his home in her bare feet, it would be quite rude to not say something.

Turning in his direction, she caught his gaze and noticed that his eyes seemed a little bluer than usual. His eyebrows were dipped down, as if he were contemplating the secrets of the universe. Her briefcase was on the floor, and Cooper was leaning up against the wall, his arms folded. Staring at her with a look in his eyes that promised things she had never seen from him before.

She almost took a step back at the sight, but knew that would be foolish. There was no reason for him to be looking at her with such intensity. At least not right at this moment. Their sexy interlude happened days ago and while she wanted to repeat it again and again, now was not the time.

He opened his mouth to say something, but she beat him to the punch. Not sure why she was concerned about what he was about to say, she only knew that she needed to fill the silence herself.

“Unless you need my help in the kitchen, the princess and I are going to go watch a movie.” Already turning toward the living room, she glanced over at him awaiting acknowledgment, “Do you need me for anything, Cooper?”

It seemed as though he took an inordinate amount of time to answer, and while he paused, she waited. For what, exactly? She wasn’t sure.

His chest rose and fell as he took a deep breath and straightened away from the wall. “Yes...I…” he began.

Arms uncrossing, he took a step toward her and stopped, shaking his head as if to clear the cobwebs. “No, I’m fine, sweetheart. You two go ahead. I’ll take care of everything for my girls tonight.” Coming over to the two of them, he leaned down to kiss his daughter on her forehead as she rested on Faith.

Lifting his face, his eyes captured hers and he paused. Her breath sped up and she was unable to break his gaze and turn away. For the briefest moment, she was tempted to lean in, ever so slightly, and touch her lips to his. Just to capture another taste of him.

To feel his tongue slide in her mouth. To feel his body press against her again. Just one more time. She wouldn’t be greedy. But with him so close, looking at her as if he wanted to devour her, she almost gave in. With his eyes boring into hers, flitting across her face as he gazed at her cradling his only child in his arms, it was so very tempting.

Couldn’t he see that she wanted this? Wanted him? Everything she had done in the last few months had to have shown him just how much she needed both of them in her life.

Ever so slowly, she saw him lean in as his gaze dropped down and focused on her parted lips. Her breath was beginning to come faster, the nervousness and anticipation beginning to course through her veins that he would close the gap and kiss her. Please, Cooper! Kiss me.

"Daddy, why are you so close to Ms. Faith? We have to go watch the princess movie." Cooper jumped back in shock. His hand came up to his face and ran along his jaw, rubbing the slight day's growth of his beard. Averting his gaze from her, he seemed upset by what he had done in front of his daughter. Well, almost done—but that was just semantics. However, what his reaction did do, was make Faith feel like a heel.

"You're right, honey, Daddy didn't mean to hold you up. You go on ahead. I'll let you know when dinner is finished." With those parting words, he turned and walked into the kitchen, away from Faith.

Bitter disappointment was all Faith felt at the moment, but she would not allow that to dampen her fun with Madison. "All right, sweetie, let's grab our favorite spot while your daddy makes dinner."

Going through the motions of getting her and Madison settled on the couch, she pulled her favorite throw from the back of the couch. Madison sat on her lap while Faith helped her take off her socks and shoes. Because this happened so often, with Faith over at their home while Cooper made dinner after a long day of work, or a lazy weekend day, they had a ritual for this, too. All of the little things they did with each other, things a family would do, made her desire for Madison's father, and his repeated rejections, whether it was to appease himself...his late wife...or even his in-laws, made the situation even harder for her to bear.

Returning her attention to the little girl wiggling her little toes like worms, Faith pulled up one foot and pretended to sniff. Giggles rose from the little girl sitting on the couch as she scrunched up her nose and waved her hand in her face. “Oh, Madison, you have stinky feet! I don’t want to smell your stinky feet. Pee-eewww, stinky feet!”

Falling back in a fit of uncontrollable laughter, Madison yelled, “This one Ms. Faith! Smell my other foot! It’s not stinky.”

“Are you sure? I don’t know, Madison. Can I trust you?” She loved this game, it brought things down to the silliest level. It was just the two of them, hanging out and doing what families do. Tears almost came to her eyes as the thought entered her head that she may never find this level of closeness, this intimacy, again. Not wanting Madison to see her tear up or cry, she quickly blinked her eyes to clear the wetness away.

With a cheeky smile, the little girl put her hands up to her mouth, as if holding back from blurting the biggest secret ever. “Yes, I’m sure. It’s okay, Ms. Faith. Go ahead. They’re not stinky!” Laughter and giggles came forward, but as a four-year old innocent, she had no idea that she was giving everything away.

“Okay, well, if you say so.” Faith lifted the other foot and pulled back in mock horror at the supposed smell. Pouncing on the little girl, she began to tickle her sides. Laughing at their game, she took on a monster voice and told Madison that it wasn’t nice to have people smell her stinky feet.

God, she loved this little girl so much.

∞ ∞ ∞ ∞ ∞

After about five more minutes of play time, she sat up and tucked Madison in next to her, the throw blanket covering the lower body of the little girl as she settled in to watch her movie. Leaning down to kiss her soft, curly hair, she pulled the little body closer. Once the movie's opening scene came on, the songs were reverberating the room. Faith's thoughts again turned to the man in the other room.

Ever since Cooper and Madison had moved into the neighborhood, her nights had been filled with visions of her and Cooper. Not just friendly dreams of going to the park. No, at night, when the lights were off and no one could see her innermost thoughts, all she dreamt about was Cooper making love to her. His lips raining kisses down her body and pleasuring her most intimate places.

Sex appeal seeped from every pore of his body, and she didn't think he fully realized it. It was more than just his outward appearance, although in reality, that would be more than enough if she only wanted to have eye-candy. No, his appeal and attractiveness came from more than that. It was that extra something which drew women to him over and over again. It was his confident, take no prisoners strut, or swagger—as the young people said nowadays. When he entered a room, he owned it. It was the most damnable thing. No matter who else was around, all heads turned to him once his presence was known.

His voice was a deep, smoky timbre. It seemed to have a hypnotic hold on her that vibrated throughout her entire body whenever he spoke. Every time he uttered even the smallest word in her presence, she would invariably feel it through her bones and the butterflies in her stomach would form a conga line.

It was almost as if he were calling out to her, beckoning her to pay attention to him, to never lose sight of where he was. Never before had that feeling come over her, even when dating someone she thought would be the one for her. No one, had made her react this way before and that scared her. Then again, maybe that's why she had been drawn to him since day one. Why she hadn't been able to walk away, even when it seemed like she should.

Hearing a noise from the kitchen, she turned her head in that direction and watched Cooper walk around to the other side of the island that was situated in the middle of his large, open kitchen. Giving Madison a quick hug, her signal that she was going to make noise, she called out, "Cooper, do you need any help?"

"No. I'm fine." Short and to the point.

Well, fine to you, too! What the hell was wrong with him? That would be the last time she would ask him if he needed help.

Her eyes lingered on the open space a little longer. He was behaving so odd tonight and she couldn't put her finger on why. Something was going on with that man and she would make sure to the get to the bottom of it.

The television called her attention again and she paid attention to the movie, for all of three minutes. Stifling a yawn, she snuggled in a little deeper. She wasn't sure how in the world children could watch a movie over and over again as if it were the first time. Looking at the rapt look of joy on Madison's face, she couldn't help but mutter, "I don't know how you do it?"

Madison's head whipped up quickly, a frown on her brow that resembled another one she had seen no more than thirty minutes earlier. Funny how such a young child could take on such adult mannerisms, "Ms. Faith! We're watching the princess!" With that pronouncement, she turned her head and leaned back into her original position. Leaving Faith with her mouth open and laughter bubbling up at the reprimand handed out from little miss bossy.

Was she being unfair to him by pushing him away? If she had been married to the person she considered her soulmate, would it be so easy for her to give him up and move on. No, she didn't think it would.

Then again, if she found someone that fit her in every other way, she was positive she would not let them get away. Call it pride, ego, or just plain selfishness, but she would not be number two, not even to a dead woman.

It had taken her too long to find out just who she was. She wouldn't give that up. Never again would she stay silent about her own needs and desires. Cooper was hers and she would fight for him, tooth and nail, even if she had to fight the memories of a woman that she had never met.

Chapter Twelve

"What the hell are you doing, man?" Mumbling to himself as he leaned over the counter, Cooper shook his head at how he was handling things.

Hands shaking and sweat rolling down his face, he was having trouble staying focused on what he was supposed to be doing. Cooper couldn't believe that he was hiding in the kitchen from a woman and his four-year old daughter. Is this what being in love again felt like? Like he couldn't breathe around her?

It had been the look on her face that did him in. Desire had been etched across her features. There had been something in her gaze that had called out to his baser needs. Almost like a siren's call that he had no willpower to resist. Her eyes had reflected a need to be taken, a hint of pleading for him to make a move.

Standing up and turning to look into the living room at Faith and Madison lying on the couch, he heard Faith call out, "Cooper, do you need any help?"

It was on the tip of his tongue to yell out to her, 'Yes. I need you to help me understand why you affect me so much. Why do I want you so much? How...how did you make me love you when I didn't want to?' Instead, he answered, "No. I'm fine."

It had been a mistake for him to give Madison a kiss while Faith was holding her. He knew better and he had almost made the biggest mistake of his life, and hers. That woman made him want to do things that were outside of his nature.

Damaged goods is what some would call him. A soldier injured on his last tour of duty in Iraq, he had returned home a different man from when he had left. His external scars had healed over time, but even to this day, he struggled with allowing anyone into his circle of trust. There had been too much loss.

His time in Iraq and Afghanistan had scarred him. The things he had seen—and had to do—in order to execute his mission, still occasionally haunted him. As the years passed, it had become easier, but the pain was still there. So many friends lost in the space of three short years. Those that had laughed with him, fought with him—gave their lives for him. That experience coupled with his misspent youth, made him a very cautious and wary man. Allowing people in was not something he was very good at.

Since his return, and after giving up his officer's commission, he had made an effort to live life differently. To live each day to the fullest.

Heather had been with him since day one and had seen him through the worst of it. Her love for him, her strength to stand by him when things got tough, had stood through the test of time. Their years together had earned her the highest place of honor in his world.

And then he lost her.

When Heather was ripped away from them, Cooper had been broken and beaten. His mind questioned how he managed to get up each day. The toll it had taken on him physically and mentally had seemed insurmountable. Raising a small child on his own had never been in the plan.

Having his wife killed by a thoughtless and reckless driver was not supposed to happen. Yet, that's where he found himself. Moving into this new home had represented a new start for him. For

Madison. A place they could call their own and make new memories, while still honoring his wife and her mother.

And then he met her and everything in his world had changed.

Noise from the living room brought him back to the present day. He heard peals of laughter from his daughter, coupled with a low chuckle from Faith. He knew it must be the scene with the girl frog and the bug. His daughter was nothing if not predictable. That movie had been played more than one-hundred times and he could almost guarantee that she laughed out loud at that scene every time.

He wondered why he still hesitated to tell Faith the full extent of how he felt. Nothing was standing in his way. Although unhappy about him seeing someone else, Heather's parents would never hold sway over his life. He respected them, but he could not live in the past. The future was waiting for him in the other room. His future was holding his daughter in her arms.

Even now, thinking back on the other night, all he could see were Faith's passion filled eyes gazing up at him. His cock hardened at the memory. She had been so open, so free with him, letting all of her need for him come out in her kisses, in her pussy grinding against him. If they had not been interrupted, he was certain he would have been balls deep inside of her within minutes. He could only imagine how tight she would feel around him while he claimed her body once and for all, coating her insides and imprinting himself all over her. He would make damn sure she never forgot just how good he made her feel.

Removing the food from the oven and turning off the heat, he walked over to the opening to the living room. His intentions were to call them in for dinner, but one look at Faith and he paused. She was asleep.

"Damn, baby, you should have said something" he whispered. He knew she had been stressed about something when she came home. And for the last two weeks she had been working late and spending all of her time away at home taking care of them.

Walking over to them, he bent down to Madison and whispered, "Hey, princess, I think Ms. Faith is really tired. How about we let her have a sleepover with us tonight?"

Looking behind her, Madison's head whipped back around and she smiled suddenly, nodding her head up and down. "Yes, Daddy, can she please stay?" She whispered back.

"Let's get you up first. Then I'll put Faith to bed and then I'll come down and we can eat," he just hoped Faith would cooperate and not demand to go home instead. "How does that sound?"

"Okay, Daddy, but be careful. She's very tired," she cautioned.

"I will, princess." Once Madison scrambled off the couch, Faith had shifted and started to wake-up, but Cooper swooped in. Bending down, he placed his arms beneath her legs and shoulders and picked her up in his arms.

"Daddy will be right back," he said to Madison as he turned toward the stairs.

Looking down at the woman cradled in his arms, he knew he was on the verge of blowing this. Of losing her. Faith would not continue to wait for him to get his shit together, and he wouldn't want her to.

It may have taken him a minute to get there, but now that he was, there was nothing that would make him give her up.

Quickly ascending the stairs, he paused in the hallway. Originally planning to lay her down in the spare bedroom, he decided against that plan. No, she would not be away from him for one more night. Faith would be sleeping in his bed tonight.

Even if he wasn't next to her, he would feel better knowing that her scent would be on his sheets. He wanted to know that when she woke up, she would be in his bed. The bed where they would eventually make love. The bed that would cushion their bodies as they finally sealed their bond. Just as he was placing her on top of the covers, her eyes opened.

"Cooper?"

"Hey, baby, you fell asleep downstairs, so I'm putting you to bed," he said calmly. Hoping that she would simply fall back asleep, he didn't want to say too much.

"Whose bed is this?" She questioned as she turned to her side and placed one hand under her head. Within seconds, she had fallen asleep again and Cooper pulled the duvet from the end of the bed and covered her sleeping form.

"Ours," he whispered. Bending down, he kissed her on the cheek.

Exiting the room, his mind was filled with thoughts of Faith and how she looked lying in his bed. He'd never seen anything sexier than her curled up, waiting for his return. The smile that spread over his face couldn't be contained. This would be one night where he and Madison would eat dinner and complete her bedtime routine very quickly. Because for the first time in a very long time, Cooper was looking forward to going to bed early.

Three hours later, Cooper found himself sitting in the wingback chair in the corner of his room. For the past hour, he had watched Faith sleep. And thought about the future they would build together. One of them would have to sell their house. Smiling to himself, he knew she would fight him tooth and nail on that. He was actually looking forward to it.

It was mostly dark in the room. The heavy bedroom drapes were pulled back and the sheer curtains allowed the moonlight to seep into the room. Watching her in the quietness of the room, he hadn't wanted to move or make any noise. Whether she wanted to or not, she was going to get some rest. Although he wanted nothing more than to climb into bed with her and pull her body close to his, he waited.

His entire life had changed in the blink of an eye and it was all because of Faith. Things had looked so bleak for him for so long. He had been worried that he was losing himself to the darkness and the only thing keeping him connected to the light had been his little girl.

Now, here he sat months later, in the semi-darkness of his bedroom and he felt at peace. Everything he needed was right here under one roof. She had given him someone to dream of a future with again. For that reason alone, he would not disrespect her and climb into his bed without her permission. Watching over the woman who made him live again, his chest felt tight at how close he had come to losing her.

No matter how long it took, he would sit here and wait for her. Until she opened her eyes and welcomed him into his bed and into her arms, he would sit and watch over her. Protect her. Love her.

Standing up from the chair, he moved to the window and looked out at the neighborhood. Street lights reflected on the street, casting the neighborhood in shadows.

It was time to let go of Heather. Madison would always know who her mother was. Her memory would be kept alive through their daughter. He would make sure of that. What they had was good and he knew that his love for her, and hers for him, had been real and true. But it was time for him to let go of the past and move toward his future. With Faith.

Goodbye, Heather.

A rustling sound came from behind him. Assuming Faith was just shifting positions, he didn't immediately turn around. Not until he heard her voice break the silence of the room.

"Cooper?"

Turning to her, he began walking over to the side of the bed, "Hi, sleepyhead."

She stretched and turned over on her back, her skirt riding up on her body from the movement. His breath hitched at the sight and he froze in place. Palms itching to touch her skin, he ached to reach out and touch her, to rub his hand along the expanse of her exposed thigh.

He chose instead to keep some distance between them, "You fell asleep on the couch and I brought you upstairs. You're worn out, sweetheart. You're not getting enough sleep, Faith."

"Oh, I'm sorry, Cooper. I didn't mean to fall asleep on you. What time is it?" She asked as she moved into a sitting position on the bed.

"It's just after ten. Madison's been in bed for a couple of hours now." Still not moving, he was afraid to do anything that would make her decide to leave.

Looking at the digital clock on his nightstand, she began to stand up, "Oh, that's not good." Her eyes took in the rest of the room, "Cooper, is this your bedroom?"

"Yes, I figured this would be the most comfortable place," he said.

Giving him an odd look, she stepped away from the bed and pointed to the restroom. "I'll be right back," she said while making her way to the room.

Cooper, didn't move. He simply turned to watch her walk away and then turned his eyes back to the window. That feeling was in his gut again, but this time he knew exactly what it meant. Tonight was a turning point in his life. Whatever decision Faith made once he said what he had to say, would be okay. It would not change the course of the path he was on. But it might force him to change tactics.

Even so, he knew that his life was going to change tonight. This time, for the better.

After a few minutes, he heard the water on in the sink for a few seconds and then Faith exited. Her skirt was wrinkled and her blouse pulled free of the waistband. Barefoot and beautiful, he looked at her with the eyes of a man in love. In that moment, he knew he would do anything and everything to keep her by his side.

Her tongue came out to wet her lips and his pants got a little tighter. Damn. "Do you want a nightshirt to sleep in?"

"Huh? Um, no, I should be leaving."

“Why is that?” Mindful of how the question may sound to her, he kept his voice low.

“Cooper, this is your bed...and your house. I should really go home. Plus, I have a long day tomorrow,” she said. Although her mouth said the words, her legs weren’t moving toward the door. Cooper took that as a good sign.

“Don’t leave, Faith,” he whispered.

The silence in the room was deafening. After what seemed like minutes, but he knew were only seconds, she responded.

“Why should I stay?” Even in the darkness of the room, he heard the surprise, and the anticipation, in her voice. Her eyes looked at him and he wanted to beat his chest and yell out to the world that she belonged to him.

“I’m asking you not to leave me. Not tonight,” his voice was husky and raw with need. “I like seeing you in my bed. I like knowing that you’re under the same roof as I am. I want nothing more than to come up to our room at night and see you lying here. I need that, Faith.” Pausing for a second, he poured all of his need for her into one sentence and prayed she would understand, “I...need...you...with...me.”

The intensity of his words surprised even him, but he knew that he had never spoken a truer statement. Finally moving over to stand in front of her, he simply took her in. Inches away from her, he looked into her eyes, allowing her to see underneath all the layers that had been built up over the years.

“Let me have you tonight,” he whispered as he bent to kiss her softly on the lips. What he didn’t say, was that he wanted her for tonight and every night after. “I need you. And you know you need me, too.”

Ever so slowly, he reached up and started to unbutton her blouse. Faith didn't move, she simply stood in the middle of his bedroom as he undressed her.

"Cooper…" she pleaded.

"Faith," he breathed out. "You have to let me do this my way, sweetheart."

"But what about…" words seemed to fail her as he brushed a kiss on top of one breast. One of his hands came up slowly to grasp the other one, his rough palm rubbing across her distended nipple. Moving his hand slightly, he brought his thumb and forefinger together and squeezed her nipple through her lacy bra. It quickly pebbled up in attention, seemingly to beg for more of the sensation.

"This is our night, Faith. Just you and me. No one else." Placing a kiss on her lips, he pressed closer to her, giving just a hint of the desire that was percolating just below the surface. "This is our beginning, baby. No more looking back. It's you and me."

Noticing the water well in her eyes, he wanted to scream out at the pain he was feeling at the moment. So much hurt he had caused her, all from his indecisions. "Don't cry, baby. I'm sorry. I never meant to hurt you."

Her body seemed to relax as she picked up the meaning of his words. "I know, Cooper. You're right, tonight it's just you and me," she whispered back to him.

Continuing his efforts, he reached around her body and unhooked her bra. All the while, he was nibbling along her lips, chin and neck. After tonight, there would be no doubt in her mind that she was all he wanted, all he needed. His life was starting over, and she would be front and center.

His head lifted and he just stared at her, looking into her eyes glazed over with lust. God, he wanted nothing more than to surge inside of her body and take her for hours. All he wanted to hear were her screams of passion. All he wanted to feel was her walls convulse as she released her cream on his cock, soaking both of them in the juices created from their love.

Love? Yeah, he sure as fuck loved this woman.

And although she hadn't said it to him in return, he didn't mind waiting. Every action, every word, every glance, proved to him that she loved him just as much. His Faith would never give so freely of herself, removing all of the barriers guarding her heart, for a man that she didn't love. Not like this.

Cooper grabbed the waistband of her skirt and pulled it down her hips. Faith's hands had been gripping his arms, but went to his shoulders when she had to step out of the garment. He threw the skirt over his shoulder, not caring where it landed. Leaning in, he placed a kiss on each of her thighs, just inches away from her moist heat.

Her intake of breath hinted at just how much she wanted this as well.

While still kneeling in front of her, he reached up and grabbed her hot pink satin underwear and pulled them down her body. The wetness from her slit could be seen as he pulled the material away from her body. Damn, he thought as his mouth watered, I can't wait to taste her. That would come later. At the moment, all he could think about was getting inside of her.

"You're so beautiful, baby. Do you know how long I've wanted this? How long I've needed you?" Loving words spilled from his mouth as he continued to place tiny kisses along the skin he had already bared to his gaze. Her thighs, the area just above her mound, her slightly rounded stomach, her beautiful firm breasts, her neck and finally her lips. Delving his tongue deeply into her mouth, she tasted so sweet to him. He would never get enough of this. Of her.

Sliding one hand down her naked body, he reached her dripping sex and was tempted to drop to his knees and lap up the juices pouring from her body, but refrained. As he felt Faith unravel as his fingers played along her slit, reaching for the bundle of nerves that would bring her such ecstasy, he refused to move away from his position. His main priority for tonight included sliding his cock inside of her and making sure he was forever imprinted on her.

He slid one finger inside of her and her mouth opened in a gasp. Rising on her toes, she tilted her body, allowing his finger to go deeper. Their kiss became messy as their passion rose and he dipped a second finger inside.

Her body seemed to suck his fingers inside and his cock began to weep with pleasure. Fighting the urge to take her standing up, he lifted her into his arms, her legs straddling his waist. Her moist heat seeping through the material of his slacks. He walked them over to his bed and laid her down. Her arms reached out for him as he went around to the foot of the bed, "Don't stop, Cooper."

"Oh, I won't. You can count on that," he growled as he quickly removed his clothes.

Her eyes got big as she saw him naked and in all of his full glory. "All for you, baby." Kneeling on the bed, he crawled up so that he was lying in between her legs. Just as he'd always dreamed of. Looking down at her, he said the words that would change everything, "I love you, Faith."

Chapter Thirteen

Heart expanding with all the words and declarations she wanted to say, Faith knew that could come later. Right now, all she could do was return the words that Cooper had given to her.

"I love you, too, Cooper," she said as he crawled toward her on the bed.

For a moment, he just stopped and stared at her. "Do you mean it?"

"I've loved you almost from the beginning. You were all I wanted or needed. My fear held me back," she responded.

Leaning back as he lay his body on top of hers, she moaned in pleasure. First contact of full body skin-on-skin and it felt like heaven. Dipping his head, he captured her lips and began kissing her as if his life depended on it. Not to be outdone, she gave just as good as she got. Her hands grabbed him and pulled tight. Her legs spread wide in abandon.

When he broke the kiss and moved to her breasts, suckling and nibbling on them, she keened in pleasure. His mouth should be labeled a lethal weapon. "Oh, Cooper, that feels so good," she couldn't hold back the gasps and moans.

She felt one of his hands moving down to the apex of her thighs and almost hyperventilated as her body tensed in anticipation. He dipped one finger between her labia, separating her slick folds with one thick digit. Rubbing the hardened nub resting between her slick labia, his finger stroked up and down, moistening itself on the juices escaping her body.

“Oh! Oh! Yes, Cooper,” she exclaimed in ecstasy.

Just then, he switched from one breast and moved to the other, his wicked mouth suckling her nipple deep into his warm mouth. Her hips swiveled and she writhed on the bed, begging for him to do something more, to go deeper. As she opened her mouth to beg and plead for release, he dipped his middle finger into her dripping core.

“Oh my God,” she almost screamed. Lifting one hand to cover her mouth to stifle the sound, she continued her litany of praise, “So good. Yes. Oh, please more.”

Cooper lifted his head from her for just a moment. “You want more,” he asked gruffly.

“Yes, always,” she whimpered. When had she ever been this needy for the touch of a man? Never. But there was always a first.

His body shifted and he gave her another deep kiss. Their tongues dueling as he continued to finger fuck her into oblivion. Nothing had ever felt this good. And then he added a second finger inside her body and her eyes flew open at the sensation. No words would come out. The only sounds in the room were the slickness of her body accepting the stroking motions of his fingers.

Faith’s stomach tightened as her body prepared for release. Cooper’s head raised as he looked at her face contort as she spiraled headlong into orgasm.

“Cooper,” she called out, “I can’t hold on.”

“Then don’t,” he rasped. “This is only the beginning. I want to see you come for me multiple times tonight. I’m nowhere near done with you.” Curling his fingers inside of her, he touched a spot that set off fireworks behind her eyes. "Come for me, Faith. Let me watch you come apart for me."

At that moment, her body responded to him unlike it had responded to anyone in the past. Lightning flowed through her body as she found release in Cooper's arms. Legs taut, her hips lifted from the bed, as she felt the orgasm pulse throughout her body, squeezing his fingers. It felt as if it lasted for hours, but eventually she began to come down.

As her butt hit the bed, Cooper repositioned himself between her legs. Lifting one knee, he placed it in the crook of his arm. Bending down to capture her lips with his, they kissed long and deep. Running her hands over his short hair, she was amazed at how strong her orgasm had been.

"That was amazing. You're amazing," she managed to say as he began kissing her neck.

"Oh, baby, just wait. It only gets better," he said on a laugh.

As he started to penetrate her with his warm thickness, she knew he had been right. Already wet and slick, she welcomed him into her body as he slowly slid inside of her. Holding him in her hand or feeling him through his clothing was nothing like this. So thick. So hot. It felt like warmed steel entering her and she almost came again right then and there.

After a few seconds of slow-going, he started placing small kisses on her face, neck and upper check. All the while, his body rocking to and fro as he widened her slick channel. Sensual words filled her ears between kisses and it made her want him more. Wrapping her legs around his waist, she became lost in the cocoon of their passion.

"Let me in baby. I won't hurt you." Thrust.

"I promise I'll never hurt you again." Pull.

"Just let me love you." Thrust.

"I'm gonna be so deep inside you," he whispered. Stopping his motion, he slowly gyrated his hips. Then he thrust again.

"Yes, more," she gasped, almost pulling back as the tip of his cock bumped her cervix.

"Almost there, baby." Pull.

"I love you, Faith," he said as he thrust again and began picking up motion. "Yeah, baby, you feel so good wrapped around me." Lifting up, he pulled both of her legs to his shoulders and began pumping inside of her. Long strokes teasing and stroking as he entered her body.

"I love you, too, Cooper. Please, don't stop," she pleaded.

"Never," he groaned as he continued to swivel his hips, bringing them both to the edge of rapture.

Unable to stop her body from responding, she felt the orgasm building. There was nothing she could do to stop it, so she simply held on for the ride. Wave after wave of pleasure rippled through her as Cooper continued to plunge inside of her body. Every thrust wringing a moan from her. Every time she felt herself tighten around him, he would slow down, lift his face and kiss her long and slow.

Once she loosened up, he would pick up the pace again. The entire time, he never stopped whispering words that filled her mind with images of them wrapped in each other's arms every night. Making love just like this.

"You're mine, Faith," he growled. "I'll never let you go," he whispered. "Can't believe I almost lost you," he ground out.

Tears rolled down her face as she realized the extent of his feelings for her. As she gave herself over to the sensation of having Cooper love her so deeply.

"I'm yours, Cooper. Always," she responded.

"I'm coming, baby. Come with me. Give it to me one more time," he said through clenched teeth as his movements became erratic.

Responding to his command, she felt another release building inside of her. His neck stretched and taut, his muscles strained, Cooper released inside of her just as she fell over into the abyss.

∞ ∞ ∞ ∞ ∞

Faith was having the nicest dream. Warm lips kissed the back of her neck while a hand rubbed her moist labia. One digit caressing the thick bundle of nerves. She could feel the slickness of her body's response coating the finger that was so determined to bring her body pleasure.

"Mmmm, Cooper," she moaned. She loved when she had these dreams. They seemed so real.

"Yes, baby, I'm right here," her dream Cooper responded.

Wait. Her dream Cooper responded? That had never happened before. As she felt the caress of a warm tongue on the skin between her neck and shoulders, her eyes popped open. Gathering her bearings, she looked at the room in front of her and it all came flooding back. She had slept with Cooper. Well, sleep wasn't quite the word she would use, considering the number of times they had made love last night.

They had christened almost every inch of his bedroom. As she thought about their interlude against the wall near the bathroom, she could feel the blush heat her skin. They had decided to take a shower after their initial two-hour lovemaking session, but just as they were coming out, Cooper had grabbed her arm.

Twisting her around, he pulled her naked, still slightly damp body against his. Feeling his hard cock press up against her stomach, she made a teeny-tiny, innocuous comment, "Looks like the little guy wants to come out and play again."

Grinning lustfully, Cooper backed her up against the wall, "I'll show you little."

"I was just teasing," she laughed. "Aren't you tired?"

"Nope," he said with a smile.

"We both have work tomorrow," she said breathlessly. Would she ever get enough of this man? Probably not.

"We can call in sick," he said easily.

"But, Cooper…," she began before he cut her off.

"No buts, woman. Well, maybe one butt," he said as he winked at her comically.

"Oh, no you don't," she laughed. "You're not going anywhere near by butt anytime soon, mister."

Pressing his body against hers as she was stuck between him and wall, he bent his knees slightly and began suckling her neck. "I'm not interested in that tonight. My goal is something else entirely."

Looking at him through a hooded, lust-filled gaze, she asked, "Oh, yeah, what's that?"

"The creamy center that's been coating my cock all night," he responded as he began to drop down to his knees in front of her.

"Oh, wow…," it had been so long since this had been done to her, but she knew how much she loved it.

"I've been wanting to do this all night," he said. Lifting one of her thick legs over his shoulder, he wrapped his arms around her ass, spreading her open to his gaze. He took one long swipe of her pussy and moaned, "Damn, baby, you taste better than I ever could have imagined."

And then that fine ass man, who had rocked her world for two fucking hours, proceeded to eat her pussy as if she were the finest meal at a five-star restaurant and he was a starving man. He left no stone unturned and for what felt like hours, he lapped, slurped, nibbled, and sucked on her until she had nothing left. By the time her fourth orgasm had roared through her body, she was speaking a foreign language.

Coming back to present, Faith closed her eyes as she replayed the memory of all they had done last night. He had played her body like a master violinist performing Tchaikovsky's Concerto with Stradivarius violin in front of the National Symphony.

"I know you're awake, Faith," Cooper said next to her, making her jump.

"Morning, Cooper," she returned, but did not face him. The things she had said to him last night had her somewhat embarrassed.

"Don't hide from me, baby. Turn around and look at me," he said, placing his hand on her hip and scooting back.

She slowly turned toward him and noticed the tray of food on the bed. Two cups of steaming coffee were sitting on the night table next to the other side of the bed. Yup, she now had proof. He was a God among men.

"Come on, sleepyhead. I made you some breakfast," he waved his arm at the spread. It's almost nine o'clock and I want all day with you.

"Oh no, I have to get ready for work," she exclaimed. "Where's Madison?" Sitting up too fast, she had forgotten about her nakedness until Cooper's eyes dipped down to her breasts.

Licking his lips, Cooper started walking around the bed, coming over to her side. "No you don't and Madison is at daycare. You slept through the hurricane of getting her dressed and off to school. There's no one here but the two of us."

Seeing the same look in his eyes that had been reflected last night, she knew she was in trouble. "No way, buster. I need to recover," the soreness in between her legs was making itself known.

"Then if you don't want round seven, I would suggest you cover those up before they become my breakfast," he said.

Grabbing the sheet, she covered her ample chest, shielding her body from his gaze. She knew it was too late to turn modest now, but still. "Can I at least get some clothes?" Considering he looked to have already gotten a jump on her in the shower department this morning, she had to at least ask. "Just something so that I can cover up?"

Shaking his head, he crossed his arms over his chest as he stood there looking like a Norse God. "No. I want you just the way you are right now. You'll need to call your office and let them know you'll be back tomorrow. Today, you're all mine and now that Madison isn't here, it's time to show you what we've both been missing."

Faith shivered in anticipation and her stomach quivered. Did he just insinuate that he was holding back last night?

Leaning against the bedpost, his blue eyes stared at her. His gaze never straying far from her, he continued to devour her with his eyes. "Go on, baby, eat your breakfast. After that, it'll be my turn," he said with a wolfish grin as he licked lips.

Instantly, her core began to clench in anticipation and wetness began to seep from her. Cooper's mouth was like nobody's business. Was he really going to have her for breakfast? Taking one look at his face and his predatory stance, she knew that's exactly what she was going to be. Breakfast.

Without another word, she reached over and picked up a bagel. It seemed she was going to need more energy. Smiling to herself as she took a bite, she wondered if Cooper could be convinced to play hooky from work tomorrow as well.

Chapter Fourteen

If someone had told him all those months ago that his beautiful, sexy, sassy neighbor would be the woman he loved, he would have called them crazy. There was no way he would have expected them to go this far. His only hope was that things between them were always as good as they were right now.

It had been a week since they had first made love and not a day went by that they weren't together. Even more than before. He was sure that Madison had picked up on the changes, but she never said anything. Plus, since she got to spend even more time with Faith, she was probably even happier.

Now here the three of them were, driving up to Delaware for a long weekend with his family. Faith sitting by his side and Madison asleep in the backseat, safely strapped into her booster seat as they cruised on the freeway. Cooper couldn't be more pleased. This is how life was expected to be.

"Don't be nervous, baby. They'll love you as much as I do," he said to her as he grabbed her hand tight within his. Faith had been looking a little green around the gills after she told him that she had changed her mind about Miami.

"No, I'm fine. I just wonder if we can keep our relationship a secret," her voice held a hint of sadncss.

"Why would we do that," he asked, genuinely confused.

"Have you ever brought anyone around your family before," she asked, turning in her seat to face him.

"Faith, you've been around my family before," he laughed.

"Not like this. Have you told them about us yet?" She quizzed him, pressing him to answer.

"No, but then again, I don't have to." He respected her concern, but he needed her to trust him on this. "I don't need to clear my romantic life with my parents, Faith."

"I'm not saying you do," she huffed, while facing front and staring out the window in silence.

"Honey, what's wrong? Something's going on in that beautiful head of yours. What is it?" Although he had an idea of the issue, he wanted her to say it. They needed to get past this.

After a few minutes, he heard her ask, "Will Heather's parents be there?"

And there it was. For some reason, she still harbored fears that he hadn't completely moved on. He had known that she still doubted whether or not he was truly and completely committed to their relationship. Seeing an exit off of the freeway, he veered over, taking them off-course.

"Cooper, what are you doing?"

"Hold on. We need to get this out in the open once and for all," he said as he pulled into a large shopping center just off the exit. Putting the truck in park, he exited and walked around to her side. Opening the door, he stood back, "Let's go. Out."

"Cooper, what are you doing? Why are you asking me to get out of the truck?"

Shaking his head, he was amazed. This fool woman thought he was mad at her. “Baby, please step out of the car. I want to talk with you and I don’t want to drive while I do it. Nor do I want little miss big ears hearing us.”

She stared at him for a few moments before moving and stepping out of the vehicle. Closing the door behind her, he raised his arms and put them on each side of her head, effectively closing her in.

“Faith, tell me something. Do you trust me?”

“Yes, of course I do,” she responded automatically.

“Do you love me?

“Yes, I love you very much. Cooper, what does…” she began, but he cut her off.

“Do you believe I love you? The truth,” he pressed.

“Cooper, I don’t understand,” she answered. He noticed that it wasn’t a response to his question, so he asked again.

“Faith, answer the question. Do you believe me when I say that I love you? That I want to be with you and only you. Do you trust me when I say that you are my future?” He waited while she just stared at him and he realized her answer was taking too long. “Faith?”

“I believe that you believe that, Cooper. I know that you want to love me. I know that it seems like I’m the one you want, but what if you change your mind? In my heart, I love you enough for both of us and I’m willing to have you for as long as I can, even if…”

Not able to take anymore, he kissed her. That was the only way he could think of to stop the words from coming out of her. Words that had no business coming from the mouth of the woman he loved. Her hands had reached up to grip his shirt, her soft moans were music to his ears. Pulling her close to him, he pressed his lower body to hers as their kiss deepened. The acceleration of a nearby car brought him back to his senses and he broke the kiss.

"You are mine. And I am yours. What we have, this thing between us is real and I will do everything in my power to prove it to you. Trust me, Faith, when I say that I love you and if I don't show you just how much I love with words and actions, then make me." Taking a deep breath, he touched his forehead to hers and spoke the words in his heart, "Oh, baby, you make me laugh, even when I don't want to. When I'm around you, I can breathe easier. I can't see my future without you in it. Yes, I was stupid and I've admitted that more times than I can count."

"Yes, you really were," she broke in, a watery smile on her face.

"And I will continue to make up for my stupidity for the rest of my life if need be. Faith, don't doubt my love for you. Don't doubt me. You make me whole and there is nothing, and no one, that compares to you. It may have taken us a while to find each other and who knows what twisted roads life has in store for us." Reaching up to grab her face in his palms, he tilted her head so that she could not look away, "I need you to have faith in me, in us."

∞ ∞ ∞ ∞ ∞

Still remembering his words to her, "I need you to have faith in me, in us," she was awed and humbled by his words. How else could she respond? What could she say to help him understand what she was feeling inside? After their little detour and Cooper's impassioned plea, she accepted that she was a goner. There was nowhere in the world that this man would go, where she would not follow.

"I do. I will. Always." After planting a kiss on her that curled her toes, he smiled at her in that sexy, 'Just wait until I get you in bed later' way and she almost melted on the spot.

"Get in the car, babe, we still have a ways to go."

Finally arriving at the Branson family vacation home, Faith took in the scene before her. It was breathtaking. Her window had been rolled down for some time and she inhaled the distinct, yet peaceful, smell of the ocean. She spied seagulls as they flew overhead in search of food. Cars and trucks were parked haphazardly around a large home with a landscaped front yard. As she craned her neck, she noticed that the home seemed to back up right to beach. However, what made her feel most comfortable, was the large group of people milling around. Kids were running around playing tag. What looked like a group of both teens and adults were playing volleyball using a well-worn volleyball net on one side of the house. All in all, it looked just like she had hoped. A family coming together to have some fun.

Cooper put the vehicle in park and looked over at her. "You ready for the onslaught?"

"I was born ready," she responded lightly.

Stepping out of the truck, Faith grabbed her purse. Going to the back door, she opened it for Madison since the child lock was engaged and she wouldn't be able to let herself out. Unbuckling her from the car seat, she peered through the window on the other side of the vehicle and watched Cooper greet his mother. Other family members started to pour out of the house and the volleyball game was paused, everyone giving hugs all around to the new arrival.

"You finally made it!"

Watching Mrs. Branson as she stood at the door, Faith heard her yell across the large yard. She watched Cooper's mom walk rapidly down the front porch steps and move toward the car.

As soon as Faith placed Madison on the ground, she took off running. "Grandma! Grandma! We made it! And see, we brought Faith," Madison couldn't hide her excitement as she made her way over to the group of people.

"Yes, I see and I'm very happy to see all of you," picking up her granddaughter in her arms, she turned to Faith who had just come around to the other side where everyone was gathered. "Come on, Faith, let's get you all settled. Most of us are on the back porch and Cooper's uncle wants to challenge him to a game of poker."

"Yes, Mrs. Branson. I'm going to help Cooper with the luggage. We'll be right behind you," she responded cheerfully. Although she had met her before on a few occasions, Faith wanted to make damn certain she was on her p's and q's this weekend.

Tilting her head to the side, she gave Faith an appraising, but not unfriendly look, "Sweetheart, we're way beyond that Mrs. Branson mess. Call me Eileen," she said. Placing Madison on the ground, she gave her a kiss on her forehead and allowed her to run free across the yard to a group of little girls calling out to her. Eileen took a few steps toward the house, but stopped and glanced back at Faith. "Or, considering how deeply my son has fallen in love with you, you can always just call me mom." And with that jaw-dropping statement, she turned and walked away from them.

Standing there looking like a fish in water, Faith's mouth opened and closed as she tried to comprehend what just happened. Turning her head to look at Cooper, she called out, "Um, Cooper?"

Pulling the bags from the back of the truck, he looked over to her, "Yeah, babe?" Closing the back, he locked the truck and walked over to her. Stopping by her side, he dropped their bags at her feet. Wrapping an arm around her waist, he pulled her close. "You okay, Faith?"

Finding her voice, she looked at him with some confusion, "Did you hear what your mom said?

"No, what did she say? Come on, let's walk inside," he said as he picked up their bags again.

"She said that you'd fallen in love with me," she was afraid to say the words into the air.

Stopping to look at her, he arched one eyebrow, "What's wrong, baby? You already know that I love you. We just talked about this, Faith."

Smiling at her in that predatory way she loved so much, he grabbed her around the waist and brought her close to him for a deep, but much too short kiss. "If you hadn't realized the truth of my feelings by now and still doubt me, then I must be doing something wrong. Don't worry, baby, I plan to make sure that I remove any doubts tonight when we're alone."

Faith couldn't help but melt at the prospect of exactly what he would do to her tonight. Once they finally broke apart, she smiled at him, "I know you do, Cooper. And I love you, too. It's stupid, but I just didn't know that she had any idea that things has changed." Rubbing her thumb across his lips, she wiped away her gloss from his lips. Standing on her toes so that he wouldn't have to bend down, she kissed him on the corner of his mouth, "I'm glad she knows. Makes things much easier. Come on, baby, let's go inside."

Making their way to the house and walking through the front door, they heard greetings from all over. Waving to everyone as they stood in the foyer, Faith saw Madison running around with another little girl, laughing as they skipped and ducked around the adults in the room. She was actually glad she had come on this trip with them.

"Babe, I'm going to go put our stuff upstairs. Are you going to be okay?" Cooper asked her as he turned to the staircase.

"Yeah, I'm fine, honey. Go on upstairs. I'll go find your mother and see if she needs help with anything," she said with a smile. After his mother's greeting, she was feeling much more relaxed about this weekend.

Weaving her way through the people milling about and relaxing, she headed toward the kitchen. She looked out the large window in the back of the house and saw Cooper's mother, Eileen, sitting on one of the deck chairs surrounded by other family members. As she approached the kitchen, she heard voices. Recognizing the voice of Heather's mother, who had just said Faith's name, she slowed down.

Not that she was trying to be sneaky, but since they were clearly talking about her, she was simply curious as to what they were saying.

"I just don't understand how Cooper could bring her with them. This is a family event and she's not family. My daughter must be turning over in her grave. That woman spending so much time with her family? She has no right. Cooper has no right to do this," she finished while shaking her head.

The other woman spoke up, "Marge, I don't think you're being fair to him. He loved your daughter, I'm sure he still does. In his own way, of course," the placating tone in the other voice was heard by Faith, even while standing so far away.

"You can guarantee that I will be speaking with Cooper about this. It is totally unacceptable to have her around my granddaughter," she said, still sounding offended.

Nostrils flared in anger, she was tempted to make her presence known. Not wanting to make a scene, but having heard more than enough, Faith walked away from the open kitchen door. Forcing a smile as she weaved her way through the large gathering of family and friends, she headed outside to get some fresh air. Exiting the front door, she took a few deep breaths as she tried to calm her temper. Anger coursed through her body, her hands shook, and her brow was furrowed in frustration.

"How dare she? Cooper is a grown man," she spoke into the air. Becoming more agitated by the second, she began pacing back and forth, waving her hands erratically as she spoke to herself. "She knows nothing about me. Nothing about my relationship with Cooper. How in the hell am I supposed to handle this."

Feeling the breeze on her face and the hearing the sounds of fun and laughter, she stopped suddenly. Why was she hiding? They had nothing to be ashamed of and they weren't doing anything wrong. There was no reason for his former mother-in-law to dislike her.

Other than the fact that she was not, nor would ever be, Heather.

The front door opened behind her and even before she heard his voice or felt his arms wrap around her body, she knew it was him.

"Hey, baby. Why are you out here," he asked.

"I'm just taking a break. There were too many people in the house," she tried to interject some happiness into her tone. She realized it didn't work when Cooper turned her around to face him.

"Whoa. What's that tone I hear? That might fool anyone else, but not me. Tell me," his dipped down and looked her in the eyes.

Not willing to keep her feelings hidden, she told him what she had overheard. At the end of her speech, she took a deep breath. "You should have told me she would be here, Cooper. I can't battle the memory of a dead woman. I can't stop her mother from wishing she were here with you instead of me."

"You don't have to, Faith. I told you before, I don't answer to her. I never have. I've respected her and Stan's feelings these past years, but that has nothing to do with us. With you and me."

"Yeah, well, tell that to her," she tilted her head toward the house. Face screwed up, she wore a look of utter frustration.

Laughing at her, Cooper kissed her on the lips and pulled her body closer to his, "Don't be mad. I'll take care of it."

"I'm not mad," she responded in a tone full of piss and vinegar. 'Okay, yes, I am. And no, you won't handle anything. We're in this together, right?" Her tone of voice dared him to say otherwise.

Turns out, Cooper is a pretty smart man after all, "Yes, together. You and me, sweetheart."

Sighing deeply, she laid her head on his chest, inhaling his uniquely masculine scent. "I won't let you go, Cooper. Not for anyone, dead or alive. You're mine. And I will never apologize for that. For loving you."

"And you don't have to. She had no right to say what she did and I—," he stopped when she lifted her head and glared at him. "I mean—we, will handle it. You are a part of my family now. Madison knows it, my mother knows it, and anyone whose opinion I care about knows it. That's all that matters to me. It should be the only thing that matters to you. Got it?"

Smiling up at him, she fell in love with him all over again. God, this man was amazing. "Got it."

"Come on, let's go back inside. Madison is in the back playing with her cousins. You and I need to put someone in her place. You with me?"

"Absolutely," she said as he released her from his arms. Grabbing her hand, he walked back into the house and went straight to the kitchen.

Standing behind him, she heard him call out to his former mother-in-law, "Marge. May I—", he stopped when she nudged him in the back. "May we have a word with you?"

Wiping her hands on a kitchen towel, she turned to Cooper with a smile. Once she saw Faith standing next to him, her smile dropped. Moving to stand beside Cooper, Faith grabbed his hand in hers and looked up at him.

"What's up, Cooper? Why do you and Faith both need to speak with me?" Her face held a note of confusion.

"Can you excuse us, Aunt Olivia?" Watching the other woman leave after giving them a smile and a thumbs up, Cooper turned back to Marge before stepping into the room, bringing Faith along with him. "Listen, I know it's hard for you to understand, but Faith isn't going anywhere. You understand that, right? Continuously bringing up Heather is not going to make me stop loving her. She's here because I want her here. I would like you to accept her in mine and Madison's life, but if you don't, then it's your loss. I'm still not giving her up," he told the shocked woman.

Lips pursed, Marge glanced from Faith to Cooper and back again. If there was anyone unhappy about their relationship, it was Marge. "Cooper, what would Heather say about this? You...you and this...woman. Dating? Are you serious? How can you have her around my granddaughter? You're a married man!" Yelling that last bit, her voice carried into the other room.

Faith felt, more than saw, heads from the other room turn in their direction. The kitchen window was open and Eileen must have heard the commotion because she excused herself and came toward the house. Entering the back door, she was about to speak when Cooper raised his hand in a signal for her to hold.

"Marge, because you're Heather's mother and Madison's grandmother, I will try to be respectful," he said in a tightly controlled voice. Gripping his hand tighter, Faith tried to share some of her support for him through her touch. "Heather is gone."

At the woman's outraged gasp, Cooper's face became a controlled mask of anger. "Are you shocked that I've accepted that your daughter, the mother of my child, and MY WIFE, is dead?" His outrage was growing each second. "I KNOW she's dead, Marge, because I was the one who had to bury her. Now you stand there and question me? You question what Heather would think of me moving on with my life almost four years after she passed away? If you knew your daughter, you would know exactly how she would feel. I honored her during our marriage and after her death. I loved her for almost half of my life." Pausing for a second, he looked down to Faith.

She mouthed, "I love you" and he smiled at her. She knew everything would be okay.

Bending his head down, he kissed her briefly on the lips, and whispered, "I love you, too." Turning back to Marge who stood in the same spot, wringing her hands, "Faith is good for me. For Madison. She loves both of us fully and unconditionally. I will not give her up simply because you cannot accept that I want to move on. It's time for me to continue living life. You can either accept it or not. Either way, I'm going to marry this woman someday. It will be up to you whether or not you have a place in our life or not."

“What? Were you going to ask me?” Faith couldn’t help but ask the question, especially considering how casually he had mentioned it.

Looking away from the frowning Marge and his mother’s smiling face, he turned to Faith and pulled her into his arms, “Would your answer be anything other than yes,” he asked.

“Well, no. But, it still would have been nice for you to ask me,” she responded.

“How about this, we go upstairs and I can make it up to you?” Smiling down at her, she recognized the look on his face and almost forgot where they were.

Whispering up at him, “We can’t do that, Cooper. Your family is looking at us. Everyone will talk.”

“So what,” he said, all but dismissing everyone in the room. “Mom, can you keep an eye on Madison for us? We’re going to go upstairs and ...unpack.”

“Cooper!” Faith couldn’t help but exclaim as she hid her face in his chest, sure that her brown face had exploded in a ferocious blush.

“Sure, honey, you two take your time,” his mother yelled out to them from her perch by the door. “Faith, honey, remember what I said to you outside? I told you so,” she quipped.

Just as they were turning around and she was being pulled out of the room, she heard Marge say behind them, “Cooper, this is not…”

Stopping where he stood, but not turning around, he said, “Marge, you and Stan are only here because my family is committed to making sure our two sides remain connected.” Facing her for a brief moment, he continued, “I care for you a great deal, but stop questioning my relationship with Faith. I will honor my past, but my future is standing right here beside me."

Faith smiled behind Cooper as he led her up to the room at the top of the stairs. Luckily most everyone else was outside or in the living room. But she was sure they would be the talk of the weekend. The old Faith would have been nervous and shy about what they were about to do, but not this new version—the new her was bold and willing to shame the Devil to get what she wanted. Walking further into the room, she sat on the bed as Cooper closed the door behind him. Pressing his back against the door, he put his hands inside his pockets and smirked.

"What are you standing there smirking for?" Taking off her shoes, she looked at him standing there and licked her lips. Damn, her man was so fucking sexy. To imagine, all those months ago, she had been feeling dejected, alone, and unloved. Not anymore. Things had changed so much.

"I'm looking at the woman I love. My future. Why shouldn't I be happy?" Pushing away from the door, he began unbuttoning his shirt. "Now, as I said, I need to make sure that I show you again, in no uncertain terms, just how much I love you. Which means, I need you to get naked. Because right now, all I need is to be inside of you."

Looking at him as he continued undressing in front of her, she didn't say a word. Lifting her hands to her blouse, she let her actions speak for her. Within seconds, she was fully unclothed and lying back on the bed. "Well, what are you waiting for?"

Epilogue

"Mommy Faith, it's time to wake up," Madison's soft voice pulled at Faith as she woke up from a deep slumber.

"Hey, sweetheart. Good morning," she said as she sat up in bed. Squinting her eyes at the bright light coming through the room, Faith turned to look at the clock and noted the time. Seeing that it was almost nine-thirty in the morning, she moved quickly to untangle herself from the bed covers. "Oh no, not today," she exclaimed. Standing up quickly, she looked down at Madison, "You're already dressed, honey? Um, where's your daddy?"

Hopping up on the bed in front of Faith, Madison swung her feet as she responded, "He's downstairs with Mimi and Papi. Mimi's cooking breakfast for everyone. Said she had energy to burn. How do you burn energy, Mommy Faith?"

"Um…" Faith was still trying to force her brain to wake up.

Not waiting for her to answer, Madison continued, "Dad said I needed to let you sleep, but I couldn't wait."

Trying not to grumble out loud when she heard that Stan and Marge were already here, Faith forced a smile, "Oh, that's good, honey" she responded distractedly. "How about this? Give me a big morning hug and then go on back downstairs. Tell daddy that I'll be down in a bit. Can you do that for me?"

"Okay, but don't tell dad I woke you up, okay?"

"I won't, sweetheart. Now go on downstairs. Make sure you eat your breakfast and drink your milk. Got it?" She said while standing at the large walk-in closet and pulling out some clothes for the day.

"Got it," Madison responded as she left the room, closing the door behind her.

Alone in the room, Faith sighed deeply as she thought about their houseguests. She knew this day would come. Six months ago, almost one-year to the day after meeting, she and Cooper had gotten married. It had been the most beautiful ceremony she could have ever imagined. Having pictured her dream wedding many times before, the real thing had come pretty damn close.

The weekend with Cooper's family had turned out to be everything she had hoped it would be. After putting his foot down with Marge, they had settled into simply enjoying the days and nights with his family. Practically everyone had welcomed Faith into the fold, except for Marge, but Faith had not been bothered and she did not allow that to steal her happiness for one second. Never once during that long weekend had she felt unwelcome or out of place. Even Stan had been nice to her, going out of his way to respect her place in Cooper's life, which she appreciated.

They had been home for two weeks when Cooper had surprised her one night. Sitting in their favorite restaurant in Arlington, VA, Faith had just returned from visiting the ladies room and grabbed her napkin to place it on her lap. Right there in front of her, in the middle of the empty place setting, was a black velvet box with the top open. Resting inside was a beautiful princess cut diamond in a platinum gold setting. Her mouth fell open in shock and her hand came up to cover her mouth, but not soon enough to hide the loud gasp that escaped. Feeling a movement by her side, she looked over to see Cooper on bended knee.

"Faith, finding you has made me whole again. The love you give to me, and to Madison, can never be replaced. I want to wake up next to you for the rest of my life. I want to argue with you, laugh with you, and make love to you every night, morning, and sometimes in the afternoon," he said with a smile. Laughter could be heard from patrons around the room who made no attempts to hide that they were eavesdropping. "Marry me, Faith. Be mine, for now and for always."

Tears fell unchecked from her face as she saw the love she felt for Cooper reflected back at her. There was no other answer, "Yes. Yes, Cooper, I'll marry you."

Sighing as she thought about her blissful, and sometimes hectic life with Cooper, she was so pleased with how life had turned out for her. While she was ready for whatever happened downstairs, she was still on edge about Marge and Stan staying at the house. No matter what Faith had done or how many overtures she made, Marge had never seemed to warm up to her. Faith knew she thought that her daughter would be forgotten or hidden away, and that wasn't something she could help her with. That was, until a few months ago. She wasn't quite sure what happened, but one day out of the blue, Marge had called. Instead of asking to speak with Madison, like usual, she had asked to speak with Faith.

That brief conversation led to more conversations, which eventually ended with Faith inviting them to stay for the weekend. It was Madison's birthday weekend and they were having a huge party at the house with all of her friends. It felt like the right time.

Walking over to the dresser, she pulled some undergarments. As she was turning away to walk into the bathroom for her shower, the sunlight caught her wedding rings and the diamonds sparkled. Smiling at the memory of her wedding day, and every day after that, her heart fluttered at the new reality that was her life. Married to the man she loved. Raising a beautiful, smart and precocious little girl. Her career continuing to flourish—after all, she had been promoted to Regional Director three months ago. Life was good now and all it had taken was that first step. A commitment that she would always be true to who she was, not the person people wanted her to be.

Surprisingly, she had even reconnected with Denise. Not that they would ever be close again like they were, but the day her assistant had put the call through, Faith had been in a forgiving mood.

"Faith Branson," she greeted into the phone as she continued to make notes on the document she was reviewing.

"Um, Faith? This is Denise."

Pausing as she listened to the one person from her past that she never thought to hear from again, Faith almost hung up. "What do you want, Denise?" Not caring one bit that her voice was filled with ice chips, she waited.

"Did you say Branson? Did you get married? Wow, that's great, Faith. Congratulations," Denise said through the connection.

The all too familiar stirrings of friendship bubbled up and she wanted to pick up where they left off. She really did. But then she remembered how they ended things. "Why are you calling me, Denise?" Faith asked, quickly running out of patience.

A pause, and then, "I'm sorry." Contrition filled her voice as Denise said the words Faith never expected.

A mere 'I'm sorry' would not cut it. Not this time. Faith said nothing.

"I miss my friend, Faith. I don't know why I said the things I did that day. You were the only person I ever trusted," Denise's voice cracked on the other side of the phone. "All I can say is that I should never have said those things to you."

"Is that all? I really have to go, Denise," she said coolly into the phone. She had wondered why she even allowed her to go on for so long.

"I'd like to start over. To build our friendship again...well, at least try to anyway. Back then, everything was just falling off the rails and I couldn't, wouldn't, see how it was my own fault." A deep sigh came through the phone, "Anyway, I'm just calling to apologize. Can we maybe meet for lunch one day soon?

Faith had agreed to think about it. After talking it over with Cooper, she had called Denise and agreed to lunch. They had talked things over and then they talked again. It had taken months before Faith was even willing to admit that she missed her old friend. She wasn't sure if they would continue to talk, but she was at least willing to give it a try.

Twenty minutes later, Faith walked down the stairs and entered the flurry of activity. Madison was talking to her grandfather, her mouth moving a mile a minute as she regaled him with her daily adventures. Cooper looked up as she walked in and came over to her. Grabbing her around the waist, he pulled her close and kissed her softly on the lips. "Good morning, Mrs. Branson."

"Good morning, Mr. Branson," she responded, looking deeply into his eyes. "Everything okay?"

"Everything is perfect now that you're here. Are you hungry?" He asked the question, never taking his eyes from her face.

"A little. Maybe some bacon and toast," she said as she peeked around him at the pile of food sitting on the counter. "Marge outdid herself, didn't she?"

"I think she's a bit nervous. This is huge for her, honey. Thank you, Faith, I know this means a lot to them," he whispered to her.

"You're welcome, Cooper. I want her to feel comfortable here. Now, let me go so I can eat," her stomach grumbled just as she said it.

Marge looked at her with a mixture of hope and sadness in her eyes. "Thank you for having us this weekend, Faith. It means a lot to us, to me, that you would welcome us in your home."

Sitting down at the table, Faith smiled at her, "Marge, your granddaughter lives here. You are always welcome." Pausing to take a drink of juice, she continued, "This all looks very good, Marge," she commented as she ate a piece of bacon.

"Um, Faith, may I have a word with you?" Marge looked nervous, but committed. She had to give it to her. The woman had went through something no mother should ever have to experience. Faith knew it was hard on her, and she tried to respect that. But

Marge needed to respect that she was Cooper's wife now.

Wiping her mouth with her napkin, she looked around and noticed Stan and Cooper about to exit the room. Madison was across the room, sitting on the floor playing with her toys, outside of hearing range. "Sure."

"Stan, Cooper, don't leave. You should hear this, too," Marge said. Wringing her hands, she looked at Faith with sorrow-filled eyes. "You have to understand. Heather was everything to us. To me. My entire world revolved around her and when she and Cooper married, and then Madison was born," pausing, she made a sound that could only be described as despair, before continuing. "My family is everything to me."

Stan came over to stand next to his wife, placing his hands on her shoulders. "Dear, are you okay?"

"Yes, I'm okay. But this is something I have to get off my chest," she smiled up at him, patting his hand.

Faith piped in, "Marge, it's okay. I understand. I never held this against you. I know this was difficult for you." Looking at Cooper, she noticed him simply staring at her with love in his eyes. He mouthed the words, 'I'm proud of you' as he watched the scene unfold.

"Faith, I was unfair to you. I couldn't see past my own hurt. It was hard for me to see how Cooper could fall in love with someone else. How my daughter could be replaced so easily," voice cracking, she paused.

"Marge, please don't do this to yourself," Faith said. Looking over at Madison again to make sure she wasn't paying attention to the adults, she continued, "There's no need for you to continue, truly." She felt horrible that this woman was humbling herself like this. This is not what she wanted.

"No, let me say this one final piece. A few months ago, Madison spent the evening with us. When I was putting her to bed, she said her prayers and I listened. My granddaughter said something that I couldn't believe. She thanked her Angel Mommy for bringing her Mommy Faith into her life. When I tucked her in, I asked her what made her say that prayer. And do you know what she told me?"

Shaking her head, Faith looked at Madison, then at Cooper. Turning her head back to Marge, "No, what did she say?"

"She said that only a Mommy that had been sent by her Angel Mommy would love her and her daddy so much. That you spoke to her Angel Mommy all the time, telling her how Madison was doing in school and how Cooper wasn't eating right." Laughing and shaking her head, "That you would do this, even when you thought no one was around to see, or judge, or question your motives, helped to open my eyes. I was wrong about you, Faith. It wasn't my place to make either you or Cooper feel guilty for finding each other. If Cooper was going to fall in love with anyone, I'm glad it was you."

Getting up from her chair, Faith went over to Marge and wrapped her arms around the older woman. "Thank you. You have no idea how much it means to hear you say that. Heather will never be forgotten and you will always be welcome in our home. You're a part of this family, just as I am." Releasing the older woman from her arms, she wiped her tears away and said, "Okay, now, let's all get ready to get this day started. We have a birthday to prepare for and a little girl to celebrate."

A smile lit up Marge's face as she clapped her hands together once and stood, wiping her tears away in the process. Yes, we have tons to do. Madison, dear, let's go pull out the decorations Papi bought for you."

As they exited the room with Madison leading the way, Faith stood at the breakfast bar. Cooper walked over to her and grabbed her face in the palm of his hands, "Hey, baby, are you okay?"

"I am."

"I'm surprised at Marge. I didn't know she had it in her," he said while pressing his body against hers.

"Well, what about our daughter? That little girl is smarter than all of us."

"Our daughter?" Cooper questioned. "You've never said that before."

Smiling, she responded, "But I've always felt it. She's as much my daughter as she is yours."

Bending his head down, he captured her lips in a deep kiss. His tongue stroking inside of her mouth, tasting her with a ferocity that usually preceded a long session of lovemaking. The sound of voices reached their ears and they split apart, both breathing heavily.

"You are not going to get us caught doing any hanky-panky. Just save that for later." Smiling to take away the sting of her words. "Don't worry, I'll take care of you when we're alone tonight."

"Yes, you sure will." Stepping away, he ran his thumb along her bottom lip and her teeth nipped his skin. "Oh, baby, be careful what you ask for. You better believe I'll remember that later. Come on, let's go prepare for our daughter's birthday."

"What will we do when we have to do two of these a year?" She asked as she trailed behind him.

Turning his head, but not stopping, Cooper had a look of confusion on his face, "Why would we need to do this twice a year?"

"Well, we can't very well not celebrate one child's birthday and not the other. That wouldn't be very fair." Faith waited as her words sunk in and Cooper gradually began to slow down until he came to a complete stop and turned to face her.

"What? Do you mean…are you...we're having a baby?" He asked, his voice was filled with disbelief and a touch of awe.

"Yes. He, or she, will be here in another eight months or so," she responded in a breathless tone. "Are you happy?"

"I'm ecstatic." Bringing her close, he let out a loud yell as he lifted her in his arms.

The front door opened and his mother stepped through just as Madison and her grandparents came running from the back. Lifting her up and twirling her around, he shared the good news, "We're having a baby!"

Madison started jumping up and down, yelling that she was going to be a big sister. Both mothers were smiling, Marge with a little moistness in her eyes, and Stan was clapping Cooper on the back. Slowly, the world around them started to fade away as she slid down the length of Cooper's body.

"Thank you, Faith. I never knew my life would change so much, so soon. Thank you for this gift, for loving me."

"You're welcome. Now, for the rest of the day, let's focus on our little girl on her special day."

"Whatever you want, baby," he said as he held her close to him.

Closing her eyes, she sent a message up to Heather, "Don't worry, you can rest now. I'll take good care of them."

Wiping away a stray tear, she joined the conversation around her, she was ready for whatever came next. Life was good. Faith was finally happy. And as long as Cooper was by her side, she was ready to take on the world.

~ THE END ~

Thank You!

To My Readers,

Thank You for purchasing Finding Faith! I hope you enjoyed the story of Cooper and Faith and their journey to finding each other. If you enjoyed what you read, please take a moment to leave a review!

Want to connect and learn more about what's going on in my world?

Main Website:
www.reanamalori.com

Facebook Author Page:
www.facebook.com/Reana.Malori.Author

Newsletter Sign-Up:
http://www.reanamalori.com/newsletter.htm

Yours,
Reana Malori

Made in the USA
Charleston, SC
08 March 2016